ALIEN'S FATE

OUTLAW PLANET MATES
EDEN EMBER

Cover by Kasmit Covers
Edited by Perfectly Plotted Books
ISBN: 9798418979933
Imprint: Independently published

CHAPTER 1

CLAIRE

Alarms blared ruthlessly, rousing me from my sleep. My heavy eyelids slowly opened and then closed quickly. Flashing lights were all around me. Where was I? Weakly, my arm hits the top of a glass encasement. Something was holding my body in place. However, there was nothing familiar.

Consciousness struggled to gain hold. Sparks flew around me, a jarring motion sending my body careening, falling freely. A bright explosion sent pieces flying in all directions. I couldn't move as I was paralyzed in place. I screamed, then everything went black.

Graduating at the top of my class, I had a degree in microbiology and I couldn't wait to use it. The opportunity of a lifetime was presented to me with a path of unknowns. I was willing to take such a risk, to be somebody both within my element and outside my comfort zone. The remote rainforest jungle in northern Brazil offered the perfect place for a brand new laboratory to study all the microorganisms in the vast tropical jungle. Imagine just stepping from the stage with a new degree in hand and being approached by the top field scientists inviting you to this once in a lifetime opportunity.

Of course, I jumped on it. After signing a five-year contract, I gave up my cell phone and the ability to contact others in the outside world so easily. Once the plane landed, I was to be taken by boat on a river for three days, and then a massive hike would follow that would last another five days to the remote lab. The pristine location had only helicopters that would drop supplies to build the lab, but no other machinery had been there since. Working off solar panels and other natural means, the remote spot in the jungle would provide all I needed during my time there. I simply couldn't wait to arrive and pull out my microscope and explore the environment.

Funny thing, a memory. Little things that happen may come to us days or weeks or even months after it happened. I ignored the butterflies in my stomach when walking through the small airport. They insisted on taking a private jet, which I thought was grand. Suddenly, a piercing pain struck the back of my neck as if something had stung me. Falling and falling, the sensation wouldn't leave.

Bits and pieces of something fluttered through my mind. Did I dream of it? What a dream if so. Someone, green I thought, stood over me. My heavy eyes could barely open.

"Sleep," they whispered.

Yes, it had to be a dream. Green aliens didn't exist. Only in books and movies. They prod and do unspeakable things to people. Yet, this seemed all too real. And I understood them. Impossible.

Gurgles and whirrs reached my ears. My head turned, and saw her right next to me. She looked at me. Dark brown eyes, dark hair, a scared expression. A tear? Surely not. Whoever she was, I couldn't hear her as her mouth moved while trying to tell me something. Reading lips made me nervous, because I never quite understood what was said.

Kelsey, my bestie all through high school, would sit across the room, mouthing at me during algebra. I would always shake my head, confused. I tried to shake my head this time, but movement seemed impossible.

The lady laid me in a pod of some sort. My arms wouldn't move. Tied down, my legs were also kept from movement. Across the room, everything blurred and melted together. Blackness again. Glorious blackness, floating in nothing, not a care in the world.

My body jolted again, a blaring alarm startled me. What was happening? Why couldn't I wake up from the nightmare? The hissing in my ears grew louder. So loud that it sounded like a million bugs flapping their little wings. Sensations rattled through my body, jolts of electricity, a stab, something. My consciousness couldn't quite grasp it.

Screams. I heard screams. The lady beside screamed too. That I could hear.

"What's happening?" I asked.

Her head shook as tears stained her eyes.

Why couldn't I turn my head? It felt like dead weight. Throbbing, aching, the loud sounds made my stomach churn. A great shudder rocked through me, the thing I was in was loosened, moved. Maybe I'll wake up. Maybe...

Riding roller coasters in my teen years gave me thrills. The sensation of rising and free-falling made me scream and laugh. I loved it. Kelsey loved it. We'd ride over and over until we felt like vomiting. I did it because I could. When I got a little older, near to graduation in college, I no longer tolerated that sort of thing. Riding roller coasters became a thing of my past. I couldn't shake the sensation.

Bright lights nearly blinded me. The air, suddenly thin, caused me to cough and retch. But I couldn't loosen the damn binds holding me in place. Whatever they were. This horrible dream or nightmare wouldn't let me wake up. I wish it had been a nightmare and that I'd wake up all snug on the plane flying to South America. I wish my reality hadn't changed so drastically.

Free-falling again. My body sailed through the air, fire flashed around me. Thunder boomed, shaking me to my core. Falling and falling and falling. Had I been on a roller coaster, this is where I would scream. But I couldn't hear my voice. Or maybe I did and I couldn't hear it outside of the noise inside my own ears.

Fuzzy images of the ground coming up fast swirled around me as I spun in the air. Then everything went black again. Mercifully. Maybe I died. Maybe I was in a coma.

"Wake up. Come on," a voice said. A garbled, deep

voice. "Come on, we've got to get you out of here. Come on, you're okay."

My eyes fluttered open. A man, er uh, *something,* stood above me talking to me. At least, I understood his deep voice and his odd accent. He wore body paint, as in all over his body, his ears, neck, chest, face, arms, hands and stomach. I couldn't see his legs. Large muscles flexed as he worked on pulling me free from whatever had me. His face leaned close, his eyes an odd green, an eye color I had never seen before, peering at me and causing butterflies to flap through my stomach.

DERIX

Not again. I looked skyward and saw the giant transport ship wavering above the outer atmosphere. Reazus Prime's gravitational pull reached far as the ship warbled. A portion of it exploded, breaking off and careening far to the west, disappearing from view. The main ship, still intact, came in low to my north. I watched in horror as it attempted to land, but as soon as it dipped into the upper atmosphere, it's hull broke apart completely. The ship exploded, sending shards and pieces flying in all directions.

I worried it would land in my canyon. Only one bit flew overhead, the fiery tail chasing it. A pod, perhaps. Whatever it was, it slammed into the side of the canyon wall, in the softer rock, breaking apart like a nest catching a baby. I wanted to ignore it and go back to scavenging. However, an inkling deep inside my heart told me to go look. Damn intuition. It always steered me right, but sometimes I had to detour to satisfy the gut feeling. This time, it grew stronger, my heart racing while I climbed down to the canyon floor and ran toward the crash site.

The pod stuck out of the side of the canyon precariously. Any slight movement and it would break loose and careen to the bottom and no doubt break into pieces. Someone was alive in the pod, my heart told me.

Reaching the pod, I saw that smoky dust covered the lid. A sound crackled through it, and the electric force went out. I had to hurry, because whoever or whatever was in the pod would run out of air quickly.

I dusted it off, and could see that an alien lay inside it, eyes closed. Reddish hair spilled over their head, and down their slight shoulders. My hands broke through the locks and the lid opened with a swoosh. The being inside took a deep breath, chest rising and falling. Female, I believe. I couldn't tell the species just yet.

My hand checked her neck for a pulse, and for an implant. Anyone coming to Reazus Prime would have an implant if they wished to communicate. The implant, freshly installed behind her ear, was covered with scabbed skin.

I tuned my implant to hers, so we could understand one another.

"Wake up. Come on," I said.

She wouldn't respond, but she was definitely

alive. I kept shaking her gently. Judging by the pod, it cushioned her fall very well, though she would likely be sore.

The pod shifted slightly, the end pointing down. I needed to get her out of it before it fell.

"Come on, we've got to get you out of here. Come on, you're okay."

Her eyes fluttered open, a look of shock crossing her beautiful face. Immediately, I felt a jolt rush through my body. The markings on my skin darkened to a deep purple, my skin glowing magenta.

"Your stasis pod is about to fall, come on, help me get you out of it," I told her.

I ripped through the belts holding her in place and pulled the lines from her veins. A bit of red blood appeared. Red-blooded, like me.

"Come on, hold onto me, I'll jump back," I pleaded.

She weakly pulled up her arms, looking at them as if she didn't know she had arms in the first place.

"Around me, come on," I encouraged.

She reluctantly grabbed hold of me, lifting her body slightly so I could push my arms around her. As quickly as I clasped onto her, I lifted her out and the pod careened to the floor of the canyon, breaking into many pieces.

The female clung to me, her neck stretching to see the mess her pod made. "I could have died," she said finally.

"Hang on," I replied as I climbed to the top of the jagged mountain and set her on a wide ledge.

"Who are you?" she asked, her breath struggling

to catch up. Perhaps it's a different atmosphere from where she had come.

"I am Derix."

"Derix, are we in Nevada? Or the desert? South America?" she asked.

My head shook. "I'm not sure where that is."

"Are you from Comic Con?"

"What's Comic Con?"

"You're painted. Like an alien or an actor in a Vegas show," she continued.

I laughed. "I'm not painted. This is my real skin. Well, up until I met you, it was all magenta. You're the alien."

The female pushed herself back, as if I had suddenly turned into a monster. "You're lying. That's just paint," she said as she reached for my skin with a hand.

I stood in front of her, showing her my body. Most of my skin showed except for my reproductive organ. I kept it covered with a fleece. Her eyes looked over my body.

"See the markings? They glow," I explained as I swallowed hard. I didn't want to face the meaning of it, but being that she's an alien, she wouldn't know anyway.

"Um, it's interesting. You're not human?" she asked.

I laughed. "Human. That's what you are? From the Terran System? Earth?"

"Uh-huh," she answered. Her face grew blank, I'm sure she was in shock. "W-where am I? South America?"

"I don't know where South America is. Is that on Earth?" I asked.

"Y-yes. Yes. Where am I?"

"Welcome to Reazus Prime. P79 Rigus System. Is this your first time off Earth?"

"Um, I've never left Earth. This is a joke, right? Where's the camera crew? You got me!" she laughed nervously and looked around.

I knelt before her. The hazy sun was setting and we needed to get out of range before the drones flew overhead looking for the remnants of the ship.

"What is your name?" I asked.

"My name? I'm Claire. I'm Claire, from Earth."

"Well, Claire from Earth, this place crawls with drones at night and we don't want to be caught by one," I said as I grabbed her hand. "Can you walk?"

She jerked her hand back. "Not *caught?* How do I know you haven't abducted me already?"

CHAPTER 2

CLAIRE

My head spun as Derix helped me climb to the bottom of the canyon. Before me, the jagged mountains spread. It certainly didn't look like anything I'd seen on Earth. The sun's eerie light made the shadows from the mountains stretch long and wide. I'm not sure what's going on, but I feel as if I am still in a nightmare.

We slipped through a crevice, the ledges too thin for our feet. Derix hopped down, his hand coming up to help me as I wavered.

"How are you able to do this?" My entire body shook with fear. Fear of heights. Fear of wherever I was.

"I've been here a while, come on."

A *while?* Finally, we reached the bottom after the scary hike down. Nothing felt real to me. I kept looking at my hands and pinching myself, hoping to wake up. Even so, I kept walking, trying to keep up with this very tall man. Alien? Surely not!

His hovel was located under a couple of large boulders and offered little for the comforts of home. Of course, I was prepared to live in a dense jungle miles from civilization in South America before the accident. This was no jungle, though. It was a weird sort of Grand Canyon, only the mountains here jutted high and ragged, the canyons deep and narrow. It made no sense.

"I'm sure we're not too different in our need for nourishment," he said as he grabbed a couple of packages from a box. "It's the best I can do. I steal food from the settlement on the river."

"So, you're a thief?" And a kidnapper. I won't change my mind on that point. How in the world did I end up in his care anyway? Oh yes; an accident.

His face scrunched in a cute way, as if he was trying to avoid sneezing. "I'm a thief only to survive. This horrible place took my ability to thrive, so I'm merely taking it back," he told me as he handed the wrapped wad to me.

"What is it?" I asked as I brought it to my nose. It smells of crackers and some sort of savory meat.

"It's breaded carameat. Easy to store. They sell it at the bakery."

"Carameat? I've never heard of it," I reply.

He poured water into a canteen and handed it to me. "Fresh from the falls." The man then told me, "The meat is from a domesticated field animal, living on the plains on Reazus Prime. Plentiful and filling. Eat."

I nibbled the wad, my mouth filling with what resembled dry biscuits and, oddly, a very beefy flavored meat. I shrug. "It could use salt."

"Salt?" He thought about the word. "Oh, seasoning. Yes, we have that from the icebergs on the ocean. I'm out of it at the moment, though. I had some on my ship, but since crashing here I've used up all my resources."

"You crashed here too?" I'm still not convinced that he didn't kidnap me.

"Yes. Four hundred and ninety-two days ago."

"How long are the days here?" I wondered, as if to believe that I am on a different planet.

"A little over fifteen hours of darkness and fourteen hours of day by Earth time," he answered.

"Earth days are twenty-four hours. More daylight and less night most of the time. Depends on the time of year. I'm not on Earth?" I shook my head. Still in disbelief, reality began to weigh heavily upon me. Even the air felt thinner here, as if there was less oxygen. I gasped suddenly.

"Slow your breath. You're okay. You haven't perished yet. Besides, they auction exotics like you here. Those have never died from breathing the air," he said.

"Other humans are here? Can you take me to them?"

"You don't understand. Reazus Prime is a prison planet. Bad things happen here. They don't care about others. The beings here are deeply involved in the slave business. Don't people disappear from Earth, never to be found again?"

I thought for a moment. "Yes," I said slowly. Yes, in fact, the disappearances always surround such mystery. It made sense in a way.

Derix didn't exactly have comfortable accommodations, his bed rolled out from under a rock. He smiled. "You can sleep here."

"Where will you sleep?" I asked as I looked around at the bare surroundings.

"I'll sleep, don't worry. The air cools a great deal at night. You'll need the blanket. You had no covers in your stasis pod."

I slid down onto the rough textured blankets, like tweed, but completely dull gray in color. "My stasis pod. I wish I could look at it again."

He chuckled. "It's in bits all over the canyon floor northeast of here."

I frowned. "I know. I'm trying to wrap my head around what's happened to me."

"What do you remember?"

I roll to my side, the cool air falling around me like cold water. I pulled the rough blanket around me to ward off the cold air.

"Not much. Bits and pieces. I thought I was dreaming. I saw another lady, in a pod beside mine. She tried to say something to me, but I couldn't hear her and I suck at reading lips," I told him as I rolled my eyes.

"What do you remember before that?" Derix perches on the ground nearby and leaned forward to see me in the dimming light.

My mind swam through the memories. "I was about to board a plane for South America. The lab had a private jet and I'm a microbiologist who was heading to work in a remote jungle. Anyway, something pierced my neck." My hand rubbed the spot and I found a scab.

Derix laughed. "That's your implant. It's why we can understand each other. Be thankful for it."

I nodded and yawned. "I'm not sure about anything anymore." My heavy eyelids began to close and sweet sleep took hold, dragging me to an odd dreamland. Maybe it's the thin air around me, or maybe I was still dreaming. But Derix, the hunky magenta alien with the deep purple glowing tattoos soon visited me. It's as if I was attracted to the alien. He drew me to him, his lips touching mine. Kissing an alien sparked a passion within me. I didn't care that I didn't know him. I wanted him.

DERIX

I watched her sleep, her mouth twitching into a smile as she sighed. I'd never been close to an exotic before. My body filled with desire and a strangeness that sunk deep into the pit of my stomach. Everything within me wanted to protect her.

Yet, her presence in my makeshift home presented me with a new problem. I don't welcome the interruption. Ever since crashing here I just wanted to repair my ship and leave this horrible place. It had been a long process, sneaking into the nearby communities to steal the parts that I needed.

I relaxed finally, my eyes growing heavy as I scanned the darkened horizon. Looking down, the color changes on my skin were obvious to me. Thankfully, they were not so obvious to the exotic. She appeared to not know that other beings existed in the galaxy. How funny to think of my race as being the only ones out here. I chuckled softly at the irony of it.

Sleep mercifully came, though my body ached from sitting against the boulder. The next morning, the Terran woman awoke with a start. Her eyes wide and wild, she peered at me.

"It's okay. You're safe," I said as I stood, stretching the stiffness from my body.

She stared up at me, her eyes gazing over my body as if she was seeing me for the first time.

"Oh yes. A crash landing. You're really not human, are you?" she asked again.

"I promise, I'm not human. I come from Aeoiz, in the neighboring system. I was flying through when my ship, *Volatus*, crashed. They tried to capture me but I evaded the guards. This isn't a friendly planet. They bring slaves in from all over the galaxy.

Her head shakes. "I just can't believe this. Derix, you're really an *alien?*"

I laughed. "*You* are really an alien. You have pale skin."

"Not all humans have pale skin. Some have darker skin, some lighter, some other hues. That's why I thought you were just in uniform. But, wow, your eyes," she commented as she stood up and stepped closer to me. "You have flecks of violet within the light blue. Amazing. Like streaks."

I peered into her eyes as well. They were the color of treetops with streaks of gold. A warm sensation rushed up my back while being so close to her. She pulled her lower lip through her white teeth as we locked eyes. Suddenly, both of us backed away. Such a strange wave of urges rushed through me at that moment, so I walked away.

"I'll be back in a little while. Stay where you are," I told her.

Her mouth gaped as I walked away.

"Wait! Please don't leave me," she begged.

"I'm getting food for us. Just wait here," I answered.

My head shook as I snuck into the community. Reaching within a pocket on my pouch, I pulled out coin currency and bought two bags of food that included freshly baked breads with melon jam and a round of jerky.

Claire rushed to me later as I approached with the food.

"Thank you. I guess I'm hungrier than I thought," she said as she took a bag.

"I paid for it," I said as I took a bite of the jerky.

"With what money?"

A smile stretched across my face. "So what if I stole it?"

"I can't believe I crashed on a planet far from Earth with an alien who steals," she replied.

Me neither. I gazed at her, the beautiful Terran with those piercing eyes, the red hair flowing haphazardly over her shoulders.

"Oh, I must look like a mess. But then you wouldn't really know what a kempt human looks like, huh?"

I chuckled. "You're stunning," I told her, hoping that I had found the correct term.

Immediately, a blush rode across her face, tinting her skin darker. "Thank you."

"Anyway, what to do with you?"

Frightened eyes widened at me. "What to do?"

"Relax, Terran. I won't hurt you." Though part of me wanted to throw her down on the stones and take her, I repressed the desire to do so. Unfortunately,my people often behaved like that. They took whoever made their skin glow. But I knew enough about the exotics not to act with brute force. Besides, I wasn't certain that I really wanted to claim her as my own. I had a good thing going, and my ship didn't lack much being repaired enough to fly off the planet and to a nearby space station for proper repair.

"I'm sorry. Really. I didn't mean to crash on your party. Just point me to the nearest village and let me figure it out," she replied.

Crash on my party? My brow furrowed while trying to understand her Earthen terms. "I'm not having a party here, I assure you."

She laughed. "It's a figure of speech."

"Oh, Aeoizians don't speak figuratively," I explained.

"Okay, sorry. I'll try to be more precise." The inflection in her voice gave me pause.

"Yeah, maybe I should figure out where to take you. Before you crashed you said you saw other humans?"

"I did. They were bound in pods like me. But the aliens..." She shuddered. "Gray, like typical aliens."

I winced. "Typical aliens, you say? To me, you're a typical alien."

"Okay, good for you. But for me, on Earth we have no clue that aliens even existed. Probably most of the population doesn't believe in aliens. There are sketches of aliens that landed in Area 51 and in Roswell, New Mexico. Smaller than you. Gray. Big black eyes. Big heads." She nodded as if I were following her.

"Could be the indigenous beings from this planet," I said.

"Oh, seriously. I guess that makes sense. So, these aliens have been coming to Earth for years?"

"I am sure that they have. This planet was once a prison planet, until a great uprising and the prisoners broke free. Now it's not a good place to visit at all."

"It wasn't my choice to come here."

"Me neither."

"Where were you going when you crashed here?"

"To other planets looking for stones to mine. On Aeoiz, I mined for minerals, but too many of my people were doing it. When I crashed here, I figured I might as well check the area for such mines."

"And?"

"And I crashed in the canyon away from civilization and since then have been on a mission to repair my ship and leave this place. I am tired of being here."

CHAPTER 3

CLAIRE

I heard Derix loud and clear. My arrival had interrupted his life of repairs and plans for escape. I get it. Though my mind spun question after question about the existence of aliens. About being kidnapped from Earth and taken to this place, wherever this place was, I understand that I am no longer anywhere near home. Still, it makes no sense to me that I could be on another planet.

I couldn't fathom aliens existing. Derix's body paint was very good, though. In my delirium last night, I thought I saw his body changing colors before me. But body paint could do that too, right? I've seen the sun change the color of some kinds of paint. That's it. My head shakes as I look around trying to figure out what to do next.

The little shelter provided little for comfort. I wasn't exactly dressed for hiking, either. The little bodysuit merely held leads over my skin while whoever had kidnapped me kept check on my vitals. Even my feet were bare. And I hated being barefooted. Too bad I didn't have my bags, for I had carried three pairs of very expensive hiking boots for my time in South America.

A pile of clothing laid behind a large stone. It was Derix's idea of a chest of drawers, I supposed. Under the clothes were a pair of clogs, or what seemed to be clogs. Sort of a mix between boots and clogs.

I slid my feet into the pair and tried walking. My feet swam in the shoes, causing my feet to twist unnaturally. No, I'd be better off going barefooted for now. Didn't the alien own a pair of socks? Anything to cover my poor feet?

A shirt made of some type of canvas, the color of watermelon meat, offered a semblance of protection over my body. I hated stealing from him, but I had no choice. I rolled up the sleeves, causing a bulky cushion around my wrists. It would have to do.

I took off in the opposite direction Derix left. It only made sense, because I wanted to leave him to his life and not be a burden any longer. Perhaps someday I could pay him for the shirt.

The steep canyon walls closed in around me. The path I chose became harder to tread. Sharp pebbles, broken from the canyon wall, pierced the bottoms of my feet. I wished I had walked around barefoot back home until my feet were calloused. Instead, my tender bottoms sparked with pain with each step. Still, I trudged onward, hoping to find some form of civilization.

The canyon turned sharply, and an outcropping of boulders offered hope to climb to the top and perhaps see a way out. The sun popped up, hotter than I had anticipated. I pulled off the shirt and tied it around my waist.

My hand grasped the edge of the boulder above me as I carefully climbed. Nerves of steel I did not have as I shook from the fear of heights. I pretended that I was climbing up a bluff over a pristine lake. If I fell, it would be into the water. It gave me courage to keep moving upward and not look down. If I had lost footing or grip, I'd certainly have fallen to my death.

I climbed and climbed and eventually reached the top. My body shook with fear as I gauged the distance to the bottom. The top offered a little surface, but not much.

"No." As far as my eye could see were more of these jagged mountains in all directions. Nothing looked familiar. Nothing compared to any terrain on Earth. Maybe Derix had spoken the truth and this wasn't Earth. What did he call it? *Reazus Prime?*

Large tears filled my eyes and rolled slowly down my face. What had I done? Even looking in the direction from which I had come, it was more of the same rugged, jagged peaks. I couldn't make out the shelter or the exact direction of it. The place seemed to morph together as one continuous blog of sharp rocks. More of the same, yet different.

The edge dropped woefully in a sheer cliff on all sides, except for the boulders I climbed. There was no choice but to retrace my steps and go back to Derix, if I could find him.

Something buzzed in the distance. Squinting, I couldn't tell, but it didn't sound like a typical plane or helicopter. Instead, it buzzed loudly and flew near. Remembering Derix's words of aliens out to enslave, I ducked quickly onto the boulder below and pressed against the wall. My heart pounded so loudly that I could barely hear the buzzing of the craft above. It hovered and moved in a way I'd never seen before.

Eerie sounds emitted from it, high pitched and bouncing off the canyon walls. My feet clamoured down another level where I could scoot under an overhang. The craft buzzed close, lowered, and then pushed the sound through the canyons behind me.

It flew fast and high and zoomed away just as quickly as it had come. My parched throat filled with gall. This had been too close for comfort. I knew I was in trouble. By the time I made it back down, I had stubbed my toe and it swelled to become angry and red.

"Damn feet. Damn shoes." The sun moved on, giving longer shadows in the deep canyon. I took off in the direction of Derix, or so I thought.

The longer I walked, the more I realized that I was lost. Where was the sharp turn I made earlier? I never came to it. Oh, Derix, where are you? Stubborn stupid me had to strike out on my own and now I was so lost and thirsty and hungry. My feet were beyond sore and bleeding. I didn't recall seeing water anywhere while on top of the ridge either. I would likely die out here from dehydration.

DERIX
My lips grumble the entire path to the hidden community on the banks of the river. A little re-

prieve between the jagged Reazus Prime mountains, it was hidden nicely between the high walls. The community thrived despite the barbarians crawling over the surface. Little known to most of the civilization, the beings here built the community while running from the slavers.

Octaurians slithered around, known for grabbing and making quick profits when it suited them. I eyed them suspiciously, though I'm sure there are bound to be those who aren't out for nefarious reasons.

"You see a pod land nearby?" the Octaurian asked.

"No, why? Another crash?" I asked as I placed the food on the counter. I always pay for some, so that when I steal more they won't suspect me.

"Yes. A large bounty coming from the pirates. Exotics were aboard, but the ship shattered upon entry. A few were caught because the pods saved them. You seen it?"

My head shakes again. "If I do, I'll let you know. I want a cut of the bounty," I told him.

"Big bounty. We saw the streak through the sky late yesterday. We're looking," he called out to me as I took my food and left.

I trekked back as quickly as I could to warn Claire and to hide her better. There was no way that I would turn her over to the pirates. They'd do unspeakable things to her, harming her in ways she never thought possible. The urge to protect her rose strong inside me, and my hearts pounded.

"Claire," I yelled out as I approached my camp, careful to point my head downward so that the sound wouldn't carry too far through the canyon walls.

She didn't soon respond, so I took off running. *"Claire?"* The camp was empty, not a sign of her anywhere. My heart pounded deep within my chest. The markings on me pulsated with a sign of trouble, my skin looking as if I had *slails* crawling over me.

The tracker within me peered at the ground, surmising that she had taken off. Perhaps to relieve herself, or maybe to run away.I wasn't certain which.

"Claire!" I shouted louder, because I needed to find her. She had a bounty on her head as one of the crash victims.

Faint, bare footprints led away, to the opposite side of the settlement on the river. She had taken the valley until she came upon the climbable bluffs. Her footprints disappeared. Carefully, I peered around the area making certain that she didn't fall.

"Claire? Are you here?"

A Stark realization flashed before me. While I was in the settlement, a drone flew around, no doubt looking for the crash victims. Oh no! What if they had caught her?

"Claire!"

There was no answer but the wind rushing between the canyon walls. The top of the bluffs offered a small surface on which to walk, but no Claire was there.

"Claire? Are you here?"

For as far as my eyes could see the vast expanse of the Raesz Mountains stretched. In all directions, it looked as if there were nothing but mountains. The settlement hid well between the steep canyon walls. One couldn't even see the river from this vantage point. My heart sank. I climbed down the opposite side, thinking that she may have done that.

I walked and yelled, and climbed back over and searched. The canyons criss-crossed, jacking off in different directions. My heart sank, I shouldn't have left her the way that I did. She needed shoes and nourishment. What if they caught her? Did I really care? If they did, I could go on with my life as planned. But I couldn't let go of the fear inside me.

The dreaded setting of the sun came, and with it icy winds began howling through the canyon. If they caught her, at least she'd be warm. But what if they hadn't? She was out there, somewhere. I had to try to find her.

I crossed back to the camp, just to make certain that she hadn't found it again. Oh, how I wished she could read Aeoizian so I could leave her a note. Bitter laughter came from my mouth as I remembered that I had no more ink sticks. I made a mental note to get one the next time I went to the settlement.

Drones flew over, their lights zigzagged across the sky. I couldn't leave the camp just yet. Claire had the sense to hide when she saw them. At least, I hoped that she did. Hunkering down, I peered up at the drones, who must have found her original crash site, or they wouldn't be searching so diligently in the area.

They moved on, deeper into the canyons, leaving

my area free. I grabbed a blanket because she'd need it. Pausing, I breathed deeply and let my intuition lead me. Aeoizians had sharp instincts of which I counted on to find Claire.

The moon hid while clouds rolled in. Great. The light on my head illuminated the path before me. An ear listened intently for the drones, and my eyes stayed keen on the skies as well. The light barely lit the path before me, but I didn't need pirates looking for Claire to spot me.

"Claire!" I kept yelling for her. I paused at the Y, trying to hone in on her. Just one meeting, and already my mind synced with her presence. In one direction, my mind was black. The other way, faded barefoot prints lit and then disappeared. It was enough for me to go on.

The night air caused me to shiver. I couldn't imagine how cold it must have made her. Fatigue settled on my body, but I kept going as I pulled out a bite of jerky and drank a long swig of water. Enough energy flowed through me to keep going.

Up ahead, I saw that the bluffs gave an easy climb to the top. My heart pounded hard within my chest. My markings glowed steadily. Yes, she was here, somewhere.

"Claire?" I called out again. I paused to listen intently. Another drone flew over as I dove to an alcove and hid, cutting out my light. The dreaded things were persistent but it gave me hope that they hadn't found her yet.

CHAPTER 4

CLAIRE

The boulder gave little comfort as I perched and gazed at the expanse of mountains before me. My arms wrapped around me provided little warmth as the last of the sun set. The sky came alive with star formations I'd never seen before. Certainly, I wasn't on Earth. Of course, South America also provided different views of the heavenlies, but this was nothing like anything I had studied.

In the distance, a bright planet arose shrouded in a haze. Close enough to look like the largest moon on Earth, only pink. It rose and set, barely showing me the beauty of it before doing so. A moon rose in the opposite sky, but clouds rolled in, blocking the light from it.

The blanket I had provided some additional warmth. It was too cold to walk on my bare feet, so I pulled it around me, tucking my feet beneath me. The stone bluffs emitted as much cold as the air blowing in and did little to help keep me warm.

A slight buzzing sound came from the distant horizon. The sound echoed through the canyons, becoming louder. Derix told me the pirates would look for me. It's the third one coming around since I first got lost.

I stood stiffly, and made my way to the edge. The slight occasional light from the moon shone above, but the canyons were shrouded in near-total darkness. Something scurried across the canyon floor and away from me. Drone lights bounced over the jagged peaks, coming closer.

"Oh no, where are the ledges?" When I first arrived, the sun sank beyond the horizon and I stayed put due to the advancing darkness. I needed to hide. The drone flew closer, dipping low in between the craggy peaks.

My foot slid as I approached the back edge. It was much closer than I had anticipated. Scrambling as best I could, I lost balance and fell backwards, hitting the boulder next to the one I was on hard. The blanket slipped down and my exposed skin stung from the abrasion of scraping against the rock.

"Oh, *help!*" I yelled. As if anyone would hear me and come to my rescue. Stupid girl, you just had to wander off when Derix wasn't looking. He did, after all, give you his bed last night. Of all the dumb mistakes I've made in my life, leaving him was one of the dumbest.

The drone flew closer so I hunkered down, my foot precariously on the ledge in front of me, the other on the one behind me. At least I was able to scoot down out of view from the top of the peak. I only hoped it was enough to hide me well. I needed the blanket, and blindly felt around for it. It probably sat on the canyon floor or hung off another ledge.

Dammit.

The drone advanced and I curled up, lowering myself and tucking my head. As if that would help, but I didn't know what else to do. My eyes squeezed shut as the drone flew directly overhead. Though the icy air sliced at my exposed skin, my palms began to sweat as my heart pounded.

Finally, the drone flew away and I dared to peek. It continued to search the deep valleys beyond me. I maneuvered around while trying to hoist myself on top of the peak again, but the ledge beneath my left foot was too narrow. I slid downward, and stopped, stuck between the two boulders. The wind sliced through, encompassing my body, further irritating the scratches on my skin.

A shaky breath didn't calm me. I couldn't see in the pitch blackness, my body precariously slipping farther down between the boulders. I was afraid to move. Afraid that if I did, I'd fall straight to my death. The boulders I had climbed earlier were steep and high.

"Please, Derix, find me," I whimpered.

Footsteps startled me. They were coming from the canyon. I wish I knew if they belonged to Derix or to a pirate. My body shifted, causing loose stones to fall and make noise. My eyes squeezed shut as I held my breath.

Suddenly, a light bounced through the darkness, slicing into the area between the boulders. Oh no! They found me. The whimper escaped.

"Claire?"

Derix's voice came from below me.

"Oh, *Derix!* I'm here. I'm stuck." I cried out because my body shifted, causing more pebbles to fall to the ground way below.

"Hold very still. How did you get like this?" He climbed up next to me.

When his light hit the cliff line, I saw the boulder behind me merely leaned toward the one in front of me. Another few inches, and I'd careen to my death.

"How did you find me?" My voice cracked.

He chuckled. "It wasn't easy. Why did you run from me?"

What could I say? "I'm not sure I was running from you or trying to figure out how to fix my situation," I replied.

He climbed very close to me. "Good thing I kept searching for you," he said with a smile.

The light on his headband nearly blinded me. My eyes squeezed shut. "I'm slipping," I said. It was more of a statement. Like my death will come soon.

"Hang on."

"Derix, I can't," I cried. My body shifted down more. The boulders widening as I slipped.

I took a deep breath, shut my eyes and gave in to my fate. I only hoped the fall would be quick and painless and that I'd die quickly.

Another inch, my head pounded.

"Oh, no you don't," Derix yelled as his giant hand came out and grabbed my hand.

My body gave way, my feet dangling beneath me. Peering up, I could see the determination in his eyes.

"Do not let go!"

He heaved and I moved upward toward him. My feet flailed helplessly beneath me. Looking down, I gasped.

"Don't look down. Look at me," Derix demanded.

My eyes swung up and locked with his. The moment seemed slowed as he silently pleaded with me. I could barely see his eyes, but the light shone on me.

"I'll save you, Claire. Don't let go," he said. His gravelly voice sent warmth through my belly. My hand tightened around his as he gently moved me from between the two boulders. I had to move in order for him to lift me to him.

"Now, reach for me with your other hand."

I reached for him, my other hand grasping his. The icy winds whipped around my body, the boulder edge digging into my flesh as he pulled me upward.

I cried as he pulled me over the edge with such force that I landed on top of him and we toppled onto the flatness of the cliff. His strong arms held me tightly as I whimpered into his shoulder. Warmth flooded my body and I didn't want to let go.

He sat upright while still hanging onto me. I stayed on his lap because I was weak and too frightened to move.

"Thank you." My voice trembled as my chin chattered from the cold.

He took off his coat and wrapped it around me. I leaned over the edge looking for the blanket.

"I'm so sorry, I dropped the blanket down there."

"You stole my blanket?" He laughed.

"I'll buy you a new one as soon as I figure out how to get my life back." My teeth chattered relentlessly.

His chest rumbled as he chuckled. "It's okay."

I settled beside him while he put his arms around me to warm me. "Now, why did you run off like that?" he asked as he pulled away from me.

"I wasn't. Or I was trying to find out if I could help myself somehow." I laid my head on his shoulder. "I'm sorry. Please, forgive me."

He makes me feel so comfortable, so at home, oddly. I couldn't help but notice the stir within me when he found me. If he didn't care he wouldn't have spent the night out looking for me the way he did.

"It's too risky trying to climb back down in the dark," Derix pointed out.

We snuggled on top of the craggy peak until the sun came up.

My eyes closed while I leaned against him. At some point, he pulled me onto his lap because my body shook violently from the cold. I didn't struggle or protest, because he gave me warmth.

The sun rose in the morning, and Derix patted my leg.

"Claire, are you awake?"

I struggled for consciousness and when fully aware, I blushed finding myself curled up on his lap. I'm sure he needed to stand and relieve himself.

"Oh, dear me. I'm so sorry," I said as I scrambled off his lap. The blanket fell from my body, my legs mostly exposed as I was still wearing one of his shirts, which had a great rip in the back.

"You got banged up last night," Derix said as he stood and helped me keep my balance.

"I'm a bit shaky on my legs. Lack of food and water," I replied. Last night, Derix gave me the water in his canteen, but I was still extremely thirsty.

"We'll head back to camp, but the pirates are out for you. They've placed a huge bounty for your capture," he explained.

I eyed him suspiciously. Now, it made sense. He wasn't after me because he cared, but he wanted the bounty which could go to fix his ship so that he could leave.

"That's why, isn't it?" I asked as I backed away from him.

"Why what?"

"You searched all night for me. The big bounty."

"What? *No!* They'd want me as well. I escaped from their prison a couple of years ago and I'm sure they'd love to throw me back in, if it even still exists," he answered.

"Why were you in prison here?"

He chuckled. "Because I came here to hunt and gather resources. They accused me of stealing and threw me into one of their prisons. A great uprising happened and the prisoners rebelled and broke out. I ran off and caught a ride with a transporter. He didn't know it, so I hid in the stockroom until he landed at a space station and then I went back home."

"But you're here now."

"Yes, because I flew too close and my ship crashed.

Over a year ago."

"I see." Still, I wondered if he was aiming to turn me in. "So you don't want the bounty on me, even though it could get you enough money to fix your ship?"

"No. If I was going to do that I would have done so when I found you. You're not the first to crash land here. Ships come from Earth all the time."

"I don't understand why not."

He laughed. "I'm not turning you in. You'll just have to trust me."

"Just point me in the right direction and I'll figure it out." I could be stubborn sometimes.

"Claire, trust me. You are an exotic Terran and wanted a large sum of money. They'll take you if they catch you."

"What are their intentions with me?"

"To sell you to the highest bidder. You'd be a slave and not just a housemaid slave," he said.

"You mean a sex slave." My head shakes.

"Yes, unfortunately. Stick with me and I'll take you to safety when I can."

Off in the direction of the rising sun, a loud buzzing drew near.

"Quick, hide."

Derix stepped onto the ledge below and helped me climb down. We scrambled down until we were underneath the ledge that leaned into the top. He took another blanket he had brought along in a pack and spread it over us.

"The blanket will camouflage us. They are out

looking for you," he said.

We were so close that I could feel his breath on my head. His great hands held the blanket over us and held me still. My heart raced as a light-headedness washed over me. Being this close to him was intoxicating. I felt woozy, or drunk, or...*something.*

DERIX

The Terran drove my instincts wild. Being under the blanket with her made my blood pump with such force in all areas of my body. Her very scent caressed my nose, causing a great urge to take her right there. Everything within me suppressed the desire.

She stirred, inhaling deeply. "They sound close."

"They are. They know the coordinates of your crash site," I replied. Thankfully she didn't crash too close to my camp.

"What am I going to do?" She's verging on panic.

I squeezed her closer to me. "Claire, what can you do? I can lead you to the community, where your image is being handed around. Do you know what it costs to send a ship to Earth? They see you as a valuable commodity. Even dead, you are valuable to them."

"What?" She started to pull away from me, but then the buzzing came so close that she shrunk into my side. I held her in place.

"Shhh, the drones are looking for heat signatures on the canyon floor, flying in between," I explained.

Her head turned to me, her arm sliding over me. "You're really protecting me from them."

"Of course, I am." I chuckle.

She lifted her chin. Though the buzzing sound is close, they aren't right beside us. My body reacts, I want her. I leaned in, touching her lips. She let me, kissing me back. The buzzing drone eventually flew away, the sound becoming faint.

We soon parted and lifted the blanket to see that it was safe. I looked at her, still sitting and looking straight ahead, as if she was horrified at what had just happened. My hand came to hers and she finally looked up into my eyes.

"Your tattoos are glowing," she told me.

I looked down, the pattern glowing a brighter magenta around my heart. *Ahem.* "Yes, that happens sometimes."

She reluctantly grabbed my hand and I pulled her to stand. "It happens. Like, it doesn't always do that." Her hand rubbed over one of the glowing designs, my body aching for more of her soft touch.

"It's a reaction."

She smiles. "These aren't tattoos at all. It's like the changing patterns on a chameleon. Interesting," she says.

"Oh, the microbiologist comes out," I say as I grin. She's quickly figuring me out.

"Yes, biologist first. Speciality in the micro part. Chameleons change to blend into their environment, especially if imminent danger is near. It takes a hormonal fight or flight to cause the reaction. But you, unless you felt that fight or flight just now with the drones?" Her eyes peer into mine. She smiles sweetly.

"You're the smart one here. You tell me," I replied.

"I don't know. You're an alien and up until the other day when I woke up while crashing on this planet, I didn't think aliens were real," she said.

"Yet, here I am. And you're the alien to me," I added and laughed.

Her brow lifts. She shook when the breeze came down from the tops of the mountains around us.

"Come, you need shoes. You won't run from me again?"

"To be honest, I don't want to run from you," she said as she caught up with me.

Neither of us spoke about the kiss. Something had certainly changed, though.

"When around a fated mate," I said as we walked along toward the camp.

"What? *Fated mate?* Surely, you jest," she replied.

"*Jest?*" My implant doesn't help me understand the meaning of some of the words in her foreign language.

She laughed at my confusion. "It means you're kidding. Joking. Telling a lie."

"Why would I lie? You wanted to know what causes my markings to glow. I'm telling you. When my kind meets their fated mate, that's how we know. What about you? What about Terrans?"

She was shocked by my words and stepped lightly as we walked over the sharp stones on the canyon floor.

"Terrans, or *humans,* which is what we're called,

have nothing remotely like that," she replied.

"Then how do you know if you've met your fated mate?"

Her mouth came open as she peered at me. I had said something that brought more surprise.

"We...we don't. We just *know.* Or we know after getting to know the other person better."

"How? There is nothing to tell you that they are the one?"

She laughed at me. "No. Humans are fickle. We can go through several *soulmates* before we find the right one. I don't know really, I haven't found a human male that fits the bill."

I smiled. "No?"

She shrugged. "I was dating my university. The biology degree meant more to me than having a man in my life."

"Yes, but what if you met the one while studying?'

Claire stopped, her intelligent eyes looking at me. "I didn't. I'm here now, so my degree is completely moot, anyway."

"Oh, I don't know. Microbiology is a universal thing. I'm sure there's an abundance of things you can do with it. Just take in new knowledge," I suggested.

Her eyes took on a far off look. "If I could have a laboratory, I would do just that. But, I don't. I'm on some prison outlaw planet, where I'm wanted as a sex slave. Seems my fate has me going in other directions," she said with a shrug.

We continued to walk along, carefully listening

and moving around the bends. She stopped and looked at me again.

"You said your markings changed when you are around your fated mate. Is she near here?"

I smiled. "She certainly is."

She gulped loudly. "What does your kind do when you figure out who your fated mate is?"

I grinned and chuckled. "We take them. We claim them. It's accepted behavior on Aeoiz."

"And the females are okay with it?"

"They feel the same urges. We don't date, as you might say. We find our fated mates and life begins anew."

"So, where is this fated mate of yours?"

I laughed. "I'm looking at her."

CHAPTER 5

Was Derix really saying that I was his fated mate? How could that even work? My microbiology mind scoured through all that I knew. If aliens were closely related to human beings, it could work. Derix looked a lot like a human, except for his skin and the strange markings.

His body ripped with muscles. He was warm-blooded, thankfully. I was even strangely drawn to him. Even his scent pulled me in and made me think things that I've never thought before. The kiss burned on my lips and hung in the back of my mind. It felt like the most natural thing to do at the time. But he's an alien. He's not from planet Earth. Could it be that there is something between us?

"Are you saying that I'm your fated mate?" The words came out of my mouth and sounded ridiculous to me. *Am* I his fated mate? Surely not.

He grinned, his eyes sparkling. "I am sure it's as much of a surprise to me as it is to you. The fact is, my markings have lain dormant all these years, my entire life. It wasn't until the moment I saw you in the pod that they lit. I don't know what to think of this either. You're not Aeoizan. You aren't receptive to me like a female from my planet would be."

I trembled. "Does this mean your instincts will kick in and you'll try to claim me as your mate?" It's a legitimate question. I don't know about his physiology and how his body reacts to such stimuli.

He laughed. "Relax, Terran, I'm not going to do something to you without your consent."

I nodded. "Okay, good. So, you actually think I'm your fated mate?"

He looked down, his brow lifting and shook his head while smiling. "I don't know what to think, honestly. My markings glow around you. That's the number one indication."

"I wish I knew how you looked before you met me. It would give me something that I could compare it to," I replied.

"The scientist in you wants to figure this out."

"Of course. I've never had anyone tell me that I'm their fated mate. I don't know what to think."

"Are you experiencing anything while being around me?"

"Obviously, there's an attraction. But you're muscular, and handsome for an alien. I'm drawn to you in some way, otherwise I wouldn't have kissed you," I told him.

"Perhaps it's true then."

"What are we supposed to do? I mean, I'm not as sure about this as you are. I just met you. I just figured out there are aliens and that I'm not on Earth anymore. My head swims with questions and curiosities." I shook my head and turned away.

Derix reached out and touched my shoulder. "Claire, I'm not going to claim you, if that's what you're worried about."

I turned back to him. "You're not. What if *I* decide that you are the one?"

He chuckled. "You're confusing."

I laughed. "Yes, I am. I can be. My scientific mind wants to know all about this. My heart, well, it's warming."

"I won't make a move unless you want me to," Derix promised again.

We walked along, the sun warmed the air, and I unbuttoned the shirt I was wearing a little. My feet were numb from walking barefooted for so long. Curiosity continued to grow in my mind as I thought about what Derix had told me. He believed that I was his fated mate. What if I gave in and allowed him to claim me? I mean, he's definitely sexy. Would something within me change as well?

I chuckled quietly at my line of thought. Surely, I was the only one in the world that puts science into everything.

"Would you claim me right here and right now if I said that you could?"

We stopped and Derix stared at me as if I had just asked the stupidest question in the world. "I'm sure I would. But I don't think you actually mean it."

This time I laughed out loud. "You are correct. I'm not ready for that. If ever. Not that I won't. I need time, dude. This is a whole new experience for me. First, I desperately need shoes."

He laughed with me. "I'll get you shoes. But you need to hide so that I can."

We finally reached the camp. I gladly sat upon the cushions of his makeshift bed, resting my poor sore feet.

He knelt before me and handed me a pouch of food. "It's not the tastiest but it's nutrition. Given that I've shown you to be my mate, you probably have similar enough genetics that you can eat the same foods as I do."

I laughed. "Okay, thank you." I didn't care. The food tasted like rice without sugar or salt, but I ate it nonetheless. A bottle of water chased it down. Derix handed me some jerky and I took a bite, savoring the saltiness of it.

"My body needs salt. Not too much, but some." The tasty jerky had plenty of salt.

"Yes, mine too," he said and smiled.

Then he took my sore bare feet and examined them. His fingers brushed over the bruises and sores. "You need bandages. And shoes." The tips of my toes rested against the tips of his fingers.

"I'm measuring your foot so I can get you shoes," he told me.

"So, you're leaving me here again, huh?"

"Unless you want to risk being spotted and having to traipse through the thorn bushes to the settlement, yes."

"I promise, I won't go anywhere. But what if a drone flies down here?"

He grabbed a cord and a light net fell over the

camp. "Camouflage. It reflects the rocks around from the outside and above. Crawl in here and put the blanket over you if one comes."

"Okay." I sighed as he got up and walked away.

Derix made me to believe that he truly cared, or why would he have examined my feet so carefully? Why would he head off to get shoes? Or, what if that's a lie and he was bringing back someone to collect the bounty? My body startled at the thought. Yet, my heart knew otherwise. Maybe he really is my fated mate? Maybe I should explore the possibilities with Derix a bit further?

DERIX

I needed to get away from Claire. Now that she knew about my changes and why, it made me want her all the more. No longer was I considering having her find another way off Reazus Prime.

The settlement was abuzz with officers from the pirate ships. Their beady eyes searched to and fro, no doubt for my potential mate. Avoiding them was futile. I might as well face them and let them know that I hadn't seen such a creature.

He shoved a three-dimensional image into my face. "Seen this Terran?"

Claire's image shone brightly before me. It was an image taken of her before she ever entered the fated ship that brought her to me. Suddenly, my heart raced as I realized that if it were not for the pirates, I would have never met Claire.

"I haven't. Terrans are rarely in these parts," I said

and gave him my best emotionless face.

"She crashed near here. She'd have shown up by now," he replied.

I looked back at the craggy peaks. "If she crashed here, it would have killed her on impact. One does not survive this place so easily."

"The Terran wasn't in the pod. She escaped."

"Or the beasts of the mountains ate her." My brow lifted. "Excuse me, I'm here on business. I don't think you'll find the Terran alive around here."

He reached out and grabbed my shoulder. "Are you a hunter?"

I turned, blinking at the pirate, whose three fingers and thumb had a good grip on my shoulder. "Yes, I am a hunter."

"You find her, you receive double the bounty," he promised.

I chuckled sarcastically. "Do you have a guarantee of this? Or am I to take you at your word?" I said as I narrowed my eyes at the being.

"I know who you are. Evading the authorities. You take my word, catch the Terran, and we give you double. I'm here until she's caught, dead or alive," he added.

"If I bought her bones for you, would I still get double?" I asked.

"Yes."

I shrugged out of his grip. "If I happen across a Terran or her carcass while I'm out hunting, I'll bring her to you," I answered.

It seemed to satisfy him for he nodded curtly

and let me go. Double the bounty. Tempting as it sounded, I would never turn over the one who was my fated mate. Lucky for Claire, I've connected to her.

I needed to know. If she really was my mate, then I need to know that it would happen. Otherwise, I could really use the double bounty to get off the planet. Spending what little I've stolen, I buy her a pair of shoes. Travel boots, with latches, so that she could climb and maneuver over the rugged land-scape. Either way, I'd claim her as my own or pos-sibly turn her over to the pirates if she didn't allow it.

CHAPTER 6

CLAIRE

Sweet sleep took me as soon as Derix left the camp. I couldn't help it. My fatigued body curled up on his pallet and fitful dreams claimed me.

Over and over, I ran from the buzzing drones. So loud, they were, and I couldn't escape them. Running from hiding spot to hiding spot, I knew it was pointless to escape Derix. Yet, if I stayed, he'd expect something sooner or later.

His kiss burned in my dreams. I turned to him, giving myself to him. He made passionate love to me, surprising me with more finesse than I'd ever experienced on Earth with a human man. Could that fact alone make it work? In my dream, I thought so.

I woke up with a start. Derix sat beside me, his eyes intent upon me. Thoughts swirled behind his sparkling eyes.

He smiled, making me feel a little more at ease. I sat up and rubbed my eyes.

"Dreaming of me, were you?" he asked with an impish smile on his face.

"What? Can you read my mind now?" I asked as I sat up fully and scooted back on the pallet.

His laughter rumbled from deep within his chest.

"No, but that answered my question. You had a smile on your face. It's good to know that I'm making you smile in your dreams."

Too eerie. "Are those shoes?" I nodded to the package in his hands.

"Yes. Travel boots. They latch so that you won't lose them," he replied.

My poor feet throbbed with the soreness of the previous day. Being barefoot was not my favorite thing. I gleefully slid my feet into the boots and instantly felt better.

"We can exchange the liners every other day or so."

I laughed this time. "On Earth, we call these socks."

"Alright. Socks or liners, you have three pairs to interchange. I won't wash them for you, though. That's for you to do," he said.

"I don't expect you to wash my laundry." I suddenly realized that I had no laundry except for the shift on my body and his shirt.

"You need clothes too." He sighed as his eyes rolled.

"Seriously? You're already tired of me? I'm sorry I crashed your party," I retorted as I stood and walked outside to find a spot for a bathroom break. In fact, I needed a bath, but I wasn't sure how the alien even bathed himself. When I returned he stared at me curiously.

"You didn't crash on my party. And I didn't have to rescue you. But I did. I know you have a need for things," he replied flatly.

"How do you bathe?" His curious expression made me smile. "How do you wash yourself?"

"Oh, yes. Bathe means wash. The river flows close by and it feeds a deep pool hidden between the canyons. That's where I bathe and wash my clothes."

I look around the camp and see a stack of folded shirts and pants. "I'm not sure where to get clothes for me, but I could wear yours. They may be a little big, but I can make do," I told him as I smiled. I didn't want to put him out anymore than I had to, but I needed something to wear.

"What's mine is yours, if you submit to me," he said with a smile.

DERIX

I laughed as I watched her face change. While I was somewhat making a joke about the situation, I was in a way serious. I was trying to see where she stood with me.

Claire nodded slowly. "I see. I need to pay for my stay. I understand, that's only fair."

I wished that I could read her better. Was she toying with me, or was she serious? Part of me thought she was serious in the way Terrans will have a relationship and then walk away. Maybe that's what we need to do, just to see. If she were to leave me once I had claimed her, I wasn't certain how I'd react. But if she was willing to pay with her body, who was I to stop her?

I stepped toward her, taking her shoulders into

my hands. "You think so?"

The Terran woman doesn't shrink back. Her brow lifted as she locked eyes with me and nodded slightly.

I closed the gap between us. A kiss would tell. My lips found hers and she responded by putting her arms around my neck. We kissed, deeply, slowly. My body came to life under her touch. Even if she was just doing it as payment, she would see in due time that we were fated mates.

It took everything I had to pull back from her. I smiled and nodded. "We need to go to the river pool so that you can wash."

"What about you?" she asked.

An invitation to join her, no doubt. "Afterward, we'll head to the spaceship and work on it," I replied without giving her an answer to her question.

At noon the pool reflected the violet sky, small clouds covering the sun in spurts. Antsy thoughts must have clouded Claire's mind, at least in the way that she kept eyeing me. I handed her a soap packet.

"Turn your back, don't look. I need to wash what I have."

"Lay it on the rocks, the fabric will dry quickly in the sun."

I turned away, chuckling to myself. Behind me, Claire undressed.

"Hey, what about you?"

"Yes, you are right. We should both undress and wash," I replied with a smile.

My clothes came off in a flash and I shoved

the garments into the water, washing and wringing them. Then I dove in while avoiding looking in Claire's direction, but I could feel her eyes burning into me.

The water splashed behind me, and I risked a turn in time to see her bend over, washing her body.

She suddenly turned and looked hard at me, her eyes fixating on my nakedness just behind her.

"What are you doing?"

"We got that over with," I said as I laughed.

She ducked into the water. "Got what over with?" Her petite body swam backwards away from me. Her arms were flailing and covering the perky mammaries on her chest.

"I figured that if we did this and saw each other, then we could get along much better. No more mystery." I swam toward her, beaming with a smile.

Claire stopped and stood, her feet on the bottom, as the water touched her chin. "Okay, I'll give you that. I'm as curious about you as you are about me. So let's do this in the name of science."

I grimaced. *"Science?* How about in the name of fate, to see if we're even more attracted without clothing."

Laughter spilled from her, so much so that I found myself joining in. She didn't move as I stepped closer, the image of her body wavy under the water.

"Derix, you're every bit as male as any human. They are driven by their cocks."

I chuckled as I looked down, seeing mine perk up to the sound of her voice. Honestly, she's not wrong.

"Except I'm not like this with just any female."

"Oh, I see, only that I'm your fated mate and that's the attraction?" Her smile reached her eyes and melted my heart.

Why wait? Why not take the daring step toward her and satisfy the urge? The closer I stepped, Claire continued to stand her ground. Nothing but the water was between us, and the desire to hold her outweighed any logic inside my head.

Our eyes locked as I closed the space between us. I had to see; I had to *know.* My hands came up and brushed against her shoulder and down her arm. She sighed, her eyes closing, a promising gesture. She turned fully toward me, stepping into my space, her chin lifted expectantly.

Sweet kisses flooded my body with desire beyond what I could have ever imagined. I groaned, my cock throbbing between my legs, brushing against her soft skin, swaying in the slight current of the water.

"Why are you making me do this now?" she asked.

"I'm not making you do anything that you don't want to, Claire," I replied.

"I have to pay you for helping me. This is the only way that I can," she explained. Leaning forward, her lips met with mine again. Passion surged between us. It was undeniable. Suddenly, she pulled back, breathing deeply.

"Let me see you." I grabbed her hand and we stepped out of the water. Our eyes remained locked. Her lips parted, the kiss burning through us.

I stood back and gazed upon her naked beauty.

Her creamy skin showed brightly against the reddish backdrop of the canyon. Perfectly curved mammaries moving with each breath she took caused me to quake with desire. The sweet spot between her legs parted just slightly. Her natural aroma drove me wild, setting my pheromones on fire. Our passion wouldn't be quieted so easily.

Her eyes took in my body, my purple cock, the swollen bulb that vibrated with desire. It was obvious, my urge to land on her and claim her. But I held back. I didn't want her giving herself to me as payment. Not really. Though at the moment, I almost didn't care. The seed within me churned, ready to burst forth and fill her sweet nectar-producing spot. I wanted badly to lay claim to her.

I smiled and nodded at her clothes. "I'm sure the fabric is dry now. Get dressed."

It took every ounce of restraint I had to turn from her and dress myself. If we're to mate, it won't be like this.

CHAPTER 7

My heart nearly thumped out of my chest at the sight of the magenta and purple god before me. His body was ripped with muscles that pulsated with desire and I wanted to satisfy him. We can call it science or we can call it mating. I didn't care. But instead, he turned and told me to get dressed.

"Why? Let me pay you," I said. It came out as if I was begging.

He chuckled, the rumble coming from deep within his muscled chest. "As much as I want to take you up on the offer, no. I'm not doing this as payment. Claire, you need to understand, my urge to mate with you isn't a frivolous passing desire. It's to mate for life. Are you ready for that kind of commitment?"

His golden eyes bored into me with such sincerity. I nearly gasped from the emotions flooding my body.

I grabbed my clothes and dressed. It's not that I don't want Derix, it's that I'm not sure it's a forever thing for me. He chuckled as he led the way back to the camp, marching in front of me.

What could I say? He wanted to be forever with me without actually knowing me. I needed to know if that's what I wanted with him; besides a horny moment of scientific curiosity.

"We need to go to a village outside of the mountains. It's risky. The ship needs parts and I'm very much wanted there. It's far enough away, so perhaps they aren't looking for Terrans from the crash there."

"How will we get there?"

"The hover shuttle, of course," he replied.

"Hover shuttle?"

"Yes, but it might be that we have to sneak aboard. We won't be the only ones traveling that way. Also, I need to disguise you so that you don't look like an exotic. Wearing my clothing will help," Derix said as he pulled out more of his clothes.

I dressed in his pants, which we turned under so that I didn't look like I was wearing clothing that was too big for me. Next, he took a rolled up blanket and stuffed it into the shirt, grinning as he stood so close that we could kiss.

"A Paldean. They are short and stocky. Rolly, even. The males are a bit taller than the females, but if we cloak in the same way as them, and somehow make your face darker, hairy, no one would guess that you're Terran."

"Not all Terrans are thin."

He laughed. "I know. But the Paldeans aren't thin at all. And they look like hairy animals."

I couldn't help but laugh. "I'm dressing as a fat bear then."

My hair was pulled back away from my face as he

fastened the cloak over my head. Wet mud and bits of stuffing from an old pillow gave me hair on my face. At least it appeared that way under the cloak. I grinned as I turned around, fat and hairy.

"Yes, you are a female Paldean. Nice. Now, I'll need to disguise myself as well, because some might know that I am wanted and would love to turn me in for invading their precious planet."

Derix drew on paper the parts needed for the ship and handed it to me.

"I'll give you enough currency to pay for the parts," he told me before we took off toward his downed ship.

"How did you get enough money to do this?"

He chuckled. "Let's just say that since landing here I've learned how to take what I need in order to escape this planet."

I couldn't imagine being stranded in a place like this for that long. "I hope I can help you."

"You will." Derix strutted before me like there were no worries in his mind.

"What if they catch me?" I asked.

He stopped, his brow furrowing. Lifting his shirt, he showed me the glowing marks. "I will go to the ends of the galaxy to save you."

It amazed me at how certain he was about me. "I mean, how do you know that I am?"

"Do we need to go through this again? Aeoizians aren't like Terrans. We know almost immediately if we've met the one for us."

"I wish humans did. I wish I was as certain as you.

It'd make everything so much easier here," I replied.

"But you have an attraction to me. Perhaps it's something you will know as time goes by."

"I do, that's true. I'm just not as certain as you are."

"Let me claim you, then you'll be sure."

My brow cocked. "Okay."

He stopped, his eyes widening. "Hmmm."

"I'm kidding. It means that I'm joking. Honestly, Derix, just a short time ago I was boarding a plane heading to South America. I woke up with you pulling me from a pod that crashed to the canyon floor. If you hadn't been there, I would be dead now."

"Exactly. Fate had me here at the right time to meet you. Don't you see that?"

My scientific mind churned. Perhaps he was right. Perhaps this was my fate. I mean, how else could I explain all that had happened to me?

"In a way."

We walked in silence the rest of the way to his crashed ship. It was hidden in the depths of the canyon under a canopy of trees growing out from the canyon wall. The *Rimora*.

"What does *Rimora* mean?"

"The explorer. It's my dream ship, and I was using it to explore the star systems out there."

"What are you looking for exactly?" I asked.

He paused and smiled, a thought apparently swimming inside his head. "For the perfect place to live."

Suddenly, as if a bolt of lightning had struck me, I realized that he hadn't found it because if this fate thing was true, he had to find me *first*. "I have a feeling that when you fix your ship, you will find this place," I told him prophetically.

"I hope so. And I hope fate has brought me exactly what I need to live a long and happy life."

DERIX

Claire's words settled into my mind as we pulled *Rimora's* hover scooter from the ship.

"Oh, it's like a motorcycle." Claire hopped on back. "What if you needed something bigger?"

"I'd rent a hover carrier."

"Interesting. I guess there's a first time for everything. On Earth, true hovercrafts don't exist. Or at least, not as far as people outside of the government know."

"Earth is far behind in technology."

"You think?" Claire held onto me tightly as I pushed the throttle forward.

"This is fun!" Her giggles sang through the air as I sped ahead, weaving through the canyons.

"Hang on, we're about to move up and out of the mountains," I told her as we turned toward the river.

The community sat at the base of the mountains, opposite the little settlement I normally visited. We traveled for a couple of hours along the main roadway that skirted around the mountains. Leaving the jagged peaks behind, we headed for the city, bustling with beings from all over. Danger undoubtedly lurked around every corner, with the pirates and hooligans out to harm others for their own gain.

Smaller ships flew in and headed toward the airfield on the top of the plateau. We pulled to the side, hiding in an alley. I didn't like the idea of sending her to the market alone, but if she walked like a Paldean as I instructed her, Claire should be fine.

"Paldean females waddle," I told her.

"Like this?" She took a few steps, her body swaying back and forth.

"Yes! You picked up on this very quickly."

She giggled. "I'm walking like a pregnant woman. That's all I can think of while wearing this fat outfit.

"You're good. Now, a being like me wouldn't be seen with one like you, so I can't walk with you. But I'll walk towards the market with you a few steps behind me. If I need to hide quickly, follow my steps."

"Yes, sir," she said as she put her hand to her forehead and waved. I recognized the military greeting. Claire apparently enjoyed playing around. It must be a Terran thing to do so at times.

The place was crawling with pirates. Many posters dotted the area in search of escaped exotics, most of them Terrans. I didn't see Claire's image among the posters, thankfully.

She waddled a few steps behind me. On the way toward the market, a shop owner stepped out and grabbed her shoulder. I spun around, staying back and listening.

"Are you Corlms?"

She shook her head. Good for her! "I am not," she said in broken Paldean language. "I'm hard of hearing." She pointed to her ears. Oh, my Terran is smart in covering her strange accent.

The shop owner let her go. A Paldean named Corlms must have visited him earlier. Claire passed for a Paldean with ease and I relaxed knowing she could purchase the items quickly and we'd be on our way back.

I paused in an alley and she stepped toward me in the dim light. "Why can't you buy this with me or do like we're doing now?"

My teeth ground together. "Because I tried buying parts earlier in the year and didn't have enough funds to cover it. I came back and stole the part, but they saw me and chased me. If I stepped back inside their shop, they'd notice me. I can't risk it."

She smiled. "What would you have done if I hadn't come along?"

I returned the grin. "That's what I've been trying to figure out this entire time."

"Fate," she said and nodded.

We moved onward, the market area crammed with beings, too many to identify.

"Two shops down, on the left. Go in and get what's on this list. Then come right back to me. I'll be right here," I promise her.

She looks into the crowd and back at me. "Okay. It looks very crowded. Don't leave me here." Claire's eyes lock with mine and I smile.

"Never."

She takes off and immediately I lose her in the crowd. The Paldean disguise hides her very well.

Behind me, a scuffle suddenly broke out. I

whipped around in time to see the same shop owner who had grabbed Claire grab another Paldean. The poor creature whimpered as he dragged her away. There was no doubt that he meant to harm her.

While looking at the busy market at the whimpering Paldean, I stepped in their direction. I could make it quick work and rescue the Paldean and be back in a flash. I know that I shouldn't, but it might help to convince Claire of what a decent Aeoizian I am.

"Stop, let her go," I said gruffly to the shop owner. He turned his hairy face toward me, meeting my stare with every bit as much gruffness.

"She owes me. Stole a morsel from my shop the other day. I'm not giving away free things," he retorted.

I reached into my belt bag and pulled out a coin and pitched it to him. In terms of the shops in town, a morsel was a small packet of food and worth far less than the coin he now held.

His eyes squinted as he released the Paldean. "Next time, she'll pay dearly if I ever see her darken my door again." The shopkeeper marched back into the store.

Her big eyes glowed at me from under her cloak. Unlike Claire, she was a real Paldean. "Are you Corlms?"

"Yes, I am. How did you know?"

I smile. "My mate and I were passing by earlier and he grabbed her thinking that she was you and called her that."

"A Paldean mated with an Aeozinian?" Her wide eyes took in my form.

I shrug. "Anything is possible on this planet. Be safe. And here, if you need help in finding food." I handed her another coin so that she could shop elsewhere for food.

One thing was for certain; most beings on this planet had to steal to survive. The coins in my belt pouch were stolen in the name of survival. I turned back to wait for Claire.

CHAPTER 8

The beings crowded in around me, and while looking back I couldn't see Derix. I sucked in a deep breath before entering the shop. Tall aliens walked about, their eyes so different from mine, peering at me with little interest. I waddled to the counter and slid the note with the items listed toward the clerk.

"Yes, we have those. One moment," the clerk said before he disappeared behind the counter. The counter was so tall that I could barely see across it. So far so good.

Someone bumped into me. I turned to see what Derix had referred to as scouts. They worked for the pirates and were on the lookout for beings like me. My head lowered so that they couldn't see my very human face, albeit disguised behind mud and fuzz from the pillow.

When I lifted my brow, bits of dried dirt fell to the floor. Note to self: do *not* lift your brow! A thousand ants seemed to be running through my veins, my hands visibly shaking.

"Here." He pushed a paper across the countertop with the fee for the parts. I handed him the currency that I had. Maybe he wouldn't notice that I couldn't count it.

I set the golden coins on the counter. "Will this cover it? Is there any left over?"

He counted out three of them and handed me

back a bronze piece. Relief flooded through me after he handed me a bag with long straps. It fitted perfectly over my body and I waddled toward the exit.

The three scouts were huddled in the corner, watching a tall female on the other side of the shop. I waddled slowly as others came in and I waited.

"Terrans spotted up the road, about that tall," one says as he nods to the female in the shop.

She's much taller than me and I chuckle quietly. They have no clue. But Terrans spotted up the road. It has to be the opposite direction of where Derix awaited me.

Outside, the sun was directly overhead, and beads of sweat formed on my body under the disguise. I looked around and couldn't see Derix, but surely he was waiting in the shadows.

"We haven't seen many Terrans here," a being said while talking with another and walking by. They both nodded back in the opposite direction of Derix.

I was in a quandary. Should I go back to Derix and have him follow me to see if it's true? Or should I go in case whoever it is has moved on by the time we get there?

The crowd decided for me as I was caught in a stream of them heading in the direction of the Terrans. *Waddle, waddle, I'm not Terran. I'm Paldean.* It was best to act as if I knew where I was going and what I was doing. As my head was pointed straight ahead, my eyes cut to the left and to the right as I looked for any signs of beings like me.

We climbed a hill, and behind me it was a mass of aliens. If I maneuvered too much, my dried mud might have fallen away from my face. Keeping my muscles from twitching wasn't easy. I wanted to scratch the dried mud that was irritating my skin.

I pushed ahead and squeezed through a small

opening toward the sidewalk and a shop overhang. It was some sort of brothel, judging by the females inside, dancing around with barely any clothes on. It was odd that they would have clear windows for all to see. Perhaps it was how they advertised.

My skin crawled as I realized this wasn't a good place for me to be. But I didn't see any Paldeans inside dancing. Short, fat creatures likely weren't allowed inside. I suppose it was probably the same in most places, the conditioning that only pretty beings, or thin ones are the best ones, was a predominant societal fact. Just like on Earth.

I saw no Terrans, though I had no doubt that they were here, arriving the same way I had. Unless they didn't survive the crash. My skin crawled as I stepped away from the brothel and headed back toward Derix.

The path winded, taking me over hills and toward some intersections. I should have found the parts shop by then as well as Derix. Instead, I was in an unfamiliar area. Nothing looked right to me. Maybe I had turned and didn't realize it? Maybe the road came to a Y at some point? As I walked toward the supposed Terrans, I couldn't see the surrounding buildings because of the disguise on my face.

Fresh tears began to fill my eyes as I went back to the building behind me. Nefarious beings searched for their exotics to kidnap and auction to the highest bidders. Dirt crumbles fell precariously from my face. Anyone looking closely enough would see what was happening; that I was not a real Paldean.

"*Derix.*" I cried under my breath while trying to figure out what to do.

The hot suns beamed down from the sky, both of them, making it feel to me as if it was twice as warm as what I would have been accustomed to on Earth.

Beneath the disguise, I was sweltering. A nice dive in the pool close to Derix's camp sounded wonderful at this point.

A cleansing deep breath helped me to think. Since I was lost, I would need to go back and search for the Terrans. Derix would hopefully come searching for me in the same area when he heard the same stories I had. In the meantime, it would also be wonderful to find others like me.

My lips were cracking from the dried mud. I needed water. These suns were too much for me. I was becoming dizzy with nausea after being so hot under the disguise. A hot woolen shirt and pants, which were turned under and doubled over my legs, were too much for Reazus' days.

A vendor stood at the corner selling glass bottles of drinks.

"Do you desire a cold drink?"

Thankfully, my implant adjusted and I understood him. "Yes, water."

I produced one of the bronze coins and handed it to him. I took the bottle and opened it before taking a drink. The cool water rolled down my throat and gave me renewed energy. A fleck of dirt fell into the bottle. Grimacing, I rubbed my hand over my face, causing more of the dried mud to fall off. Using the water, I washed the remainder of the mud and fuzz from my face. I would merely keep the cloak over my features and hope that the shadow would hide me.

DERIX

Too much time had elapsed and Claire hadn't shown up. Squaring my shoulders, I moved toward the market square where she should have bought the parts and returned. Streams of beings packed the streets with no room for any traveling craft. This was a good thing. Claire was nowhere in sight.

Three pirates stood outside the parts shop, huddled and talking low. I stepped closer to them and listened to their conversation.

"Two. One is Terran. Found wandering after the crash."

My hands balled into fists.

One of them looked at a three-dimensional comm list hovering over his wrist. "Twelve found, three dead."

Twelve found. I was certain that there were more than twelve aboard Claire's ship. I'm not certain, however, if Claire was among their total count.

I pulled down my hood, which was very similar to what many beings in the market wore when the hot suns were overhead like they were now. It allowed me some cover as I stepped into the parts shop. Luckily, it was packed with customers and no one took notice of me. More pirates were inside, busily discussing the Terran they had just captured.

Claire wasn't there. Did they take her? Heading back outside, I stepped far enough away from the pirates congregating together and strained to hear their conversation while hoping that they wouldn't notice me.

Nothing indicated where she might be, so I took

off in the opposite direction. I saw no Terrans along the way as the crowd moved along the street. There were so many of them. I wondered why they were all crowding into the markets. This place had always been busy, but today it was even busier than usual. Chills clawed down my back at the realization of a possible auction occurring today. The pirates scoured the area for beings to kidnap, no doubt. Females of all races were in danger here.

Poor Claire. She must have been frightened. Regret hung off me like the doom of an impending crash, which I know all too well. I should have gone with her. I should have at least waited just outside the door where I could have looked inside from the road.

The slight Y in the road could confuse anyone who didn't know the area. If Claire had gotten caught up in the throng as it was walking, it would have been easy for her to get turned around. To my horror, I came to the slight Y in the road. Instinct had me to turn in one particular direction.

Oh, Claire, where are you? To have come this far in life, crashing on Reazus and then having my fated mate crash into my arms seemed impossible. And now she seemed to have disappeared from the city.

Every shop I scoured came up empty. Every road in this forsaken city I searched came up empty. No Claire. What if she somehow had gotten away and gone back to the camp? We were two hours away by vehicle. If she had run, she'd have been on the road.

I retraced my steps, double checking each shop

and drinking joint, even the parts shop again. Slowly, I realized that I had no choice but to make my way back to the hovercraft. The two suns were setting, light streaks crisscrossing as the shadows darkened.

The canyons loomed ahead, eerily quiet. I would have been relieved if I had seen a drone scouting the area again. That would have meant that Claire was still out there. Darkness closed in as I slowly drove, my ears listening intently for any sounds.

"Claire?" My voice boomed ahead as I paused along the side of the road. Only the echo of her name answered back.

My beautiful Terran, so close, so ready for me, and now gone. Deep canyon walls lined the sides of the road. Each one I checked came up empty. There was nothing but darkness.

Light flickered from my camp, my heart surging with hope.

"No." The lights from the hovercraft reflected from a metallic box poking out from under the netting. She was not there.

Icy air descended into the deep valleys, swirling the threat of freezing temperatures. I gazed around, wishing that she'd walk up. The indentation of her head still shaped my pillow. Bringing it to my nose, I could smell her. A chill rushed through me and I couldn't lie down and sleep. Claire was out there and she needed me.

I took the path back to the city, driving slowly and straining to see in the darkness for any signs

of Claire. Thunder rumbled in the distance, bringing in the threat of icy roads, which would turn into
flooded areas by the next day. It was becoming pro-
gressively more dangerous for her to be out on her
own.

City lights beamed into the sky, a place where no
one slept. Paldeans came out more at night due to
their need for cooler air. Each one that passed, I look
at with great interest.

"Claire," I called as I edged through the crowd. No
one turned around or answered me. My heart sank;
she was not among them.

The parts shop was dark, closed for the night.
Everywhere there were cameras that recorded
things. An Aeoizian such as me looking into a darkened closed shop would cause alarm.

I headed back and grabbed the craft and drove to
the other side of the city by traveling around another road. It wasn't at all very smart, but I needed
to know. A group of pirates were congregated at the
head of a well-guarded road. I pulled up and nodded
to one.

"Yes?"

"Where is the auction house?"

"Interested in a slave?"

I nodded.

"What kind?"

A grin stretched across my face. "The kind I can
claim," I said huskily.

He returned the smile. "Good. Tomorrow at sun-
set. Straight down. You can't enter except with a gal-

actic currency card."

The other pirate toward me. "Fully loaded if you want an exotic," he said and then nodded.

"Thank you."

I left with a heavy heart. The funds I had were stolen already, and I didn't have a galactic currency card. The roads would be heavy with traffic tomorrow. I planned to find a way to get inside without the card. I would do anything for Claire.

The empty camp broke my heart when I returned again. If Claire was in their custody, she would be put on auction tomorrow. If not, I wasn't sure what I would do. I had a strong feeling that I would find her at the heavily guarded auction house, though.

The next morning, the first sun rose, bathing the area in pinkish light because of the icy storm from last night. By the time the second sun arose, the ice melted, leaving masses of puddles and streams running throughout the canyons. No matter the mucky mess around me, I would go and find my mate. I would swear my life to it.

CHAPTER 9

CLAIRE

It happened so quickly. My world was turned upside down again. I turned to head back in the opposite direction, thinking that I might find Derix, and ran smack into a hulking being. At first, I thought it was Derix, but then large hands with long spindly fingers grabbed me and a hood came over my head.

"Stop! Let me go!" I screamed. Though I struggled, the hands had a tight grip on me. My value to them seemed far too great and others around seemed not to care that a slight being such as myself screamed for help.

The more I struggled, the tighter their grips. My body was bent forcibly and shoved into a small container. No matter how loud I shrieked, no one came to help me.

I was in a vehicle, riding over the bumpy road, the container jarring. My life flashed before me, so many things having happened to me in the last month, I couldn't keep up. Thoughts crashed upon me like the white rapids of a raging river. Now, the only semblance of something I liked, something of comfort, was gone.

"Derix." I cried softly.

Nothing good would come from my being captured. It was the very reason why I was on Reazus in the first place. Now my captors would see fit to sell me to the highest bidder.

The vehicle suddenly stopped. I couldn't hear anything outside, but my heart was pounding inside my ears.

A blinding light struck my eyes as the container door opened. I blinked at whoever held the light, my hand coming up to shield my eyes. I shook my head as the babble of words came at me. I did not understand. They leaned forward and tapped the implant behind my ear. Temporary pain rushed through my head as I grimaced.

The hood of my disguise came off when someone behind me yanked up on it. I spun around, seeing another being like the one in front of me. Vertical eyes blinked sideways at 180 degrees to mine. Two holes for nostrils and a tiny mouth from which to utter high pitched sounds were also visible on their faces.

"What are you?" they asked.

"What are you?" I was proud of the way that I countered. I hid the smile stretching across my face.

"We are Protus. Daet, come," one said.

Daet, another Protus, stepped into the small room and blinked at me.

"Ah, what extraordinary bounty we have. A Terran!"

My head shook vehemently. "No, I'm not. I'm Paldean," I told him. The pillow and large woolen cloak was on my body, giving me the appearance of being plump.

"No, Feda, they are Terran. Change the covers," Daet replied.

The two Protus beings lifted me to my feet, forcing me to march ahead of them through a long hall. My waddling steps did little to convince them otherwise. With a shove, I nearly tripped into what I would guess was a female Protus.

Her eyes were larger with longer eyelashes, curled back. It reminded me of the eyelashes people would put on their car's headlights back on Earth. Only hers were real.

"Come. Off with covers," she said to me.

My brow furrowed. "I don't have covers?"

"This." She pulled at my cloak. I backed away.

"No, I'm not removing my clothes."

She turned and pulled a garment from the closet behind her. A cornflower blue dress made of filmy material. It resembled an evening gown found on Earth, which surprised me.

"Wear this. We need to see you," she continued.

My head shook. "No thank you," I answered.

"If you don't do it, we'll force you." Her matter-of-fact words came out very calmly,but the threat was very real.

"Why?"

"Do it. For your benefit to obey." Clearly, I was losing the battle over my clothing. Still, I didn't remove my cloak, trying to maintain that I was Paldean.

"Oate."

The same one who grabbed me earlier came into

the room. Both Oate and the female roughly yanked on the cloak I was wearing. The pillow spilled onto the floor and elicited rumbles of laughter. Strength overpowered me and the rest of my outfit came off.

"Dealeth do it," Oate demanded.

She shoved the dress over my head, the filmy material clinging to my curves.

"Terran."

"Disguise."

My head lowered, defeated and at the mercy of these Protus beings.

"I have a mate," I told them after some thought.

"A mate who thought he claimed a Paldean?" Dealeth laughed.

"No. He knows what I am. He'll come for me. He's a warrior," I said.

Their laughter sickened my stomach.

"Never again. You have new master soon. Far valuable."

Even though they spoke in broken sentences to my ears, I understood every word. My curiosity of looking for the other Terrans had put me in extreme danger and now I would very likely never see Derix again.

"Please, let me go. I won't be any good for a master. I'm damaged goods."

"Why?" Dealeth held out her hands at me.

"I can't have children." I lied. Make it up, lie and get out of it.

"You can't? Not all want children."

"I won't bring top dollar if I'm damaged. I lost my

female organs to cancer," I lied.

Dealeth narrowed her eyes at me. "You're young for disease." Her head shook. Funny how certain actions were universal.

It didn't matter anyway, the Protus didn't believe me. Wearing nothing but the thin blue dress, they marched me down another long hall and into a holding cell with other beings. But no Terrans.

I slid against a wall, sitting, a draft of cold air settling upon me. Each female looked at me sorrowfully. The guards stood outside the doors watching.

"Can anyone understand me?"

"You, back there, Terran. Keep your mouth shut or we'll put you in the dungeon alone with the vermeias."

"What's a *vermeia?*" I whispered to another captive.

"Like critea, only bigger," said the female beside me. Her height could overshadow any male on Earth and her accent sounded strongly Russian, but I knew better.

My body trembled as I hugged myself. I decided to keep quiet and stay away from the vermeias.

CHAPTER 10

DERIX

My feet made huge indentations in the mud as I stomped into the city, walking in line with the other captives. The energy of the day came from all the races present at the same time, each with different missions. Some were pirates, there to exploit others for their own gain. Others were old prisoners who were trying to carve out a new life. And yet more were there for the express purpose of the upcoming auction that promised exotics for sale.

My nostrils flared as I searched through the streets for anyone remotely looking like a Terran. If it took me the rest of my life to find her, so be it. It was my fault that she had gotten lost or grabbed. It was my fault that I didn't follow her all the way to the shop in the first place. Too many questions flowed through my head, as I was determined to find her.

Most importantly, I needed a currency card with enough funds on it to purchase Claire should she end up on the auction floor. Opes district had the best opportunities for grabbing a large currency card. Only the wealthiest shopped in the Opes district, a place I rarely went.

Highly influential beings strolled the avenues of Opes, buying the best. My eyes widened at the ridiculous prices in the shops for clothing and everyday merchandise. The largest crowd there surrounded a cart of jewelry. They were made up of jewels that were mined from a giant asteroid flying through the P79 Rigus System. Anyone around the cart would have high currency cards, because the star jewels were extremely expensive to purchase.

I bumped through the crowd, my hands moving swiftly as I swiped several cards that were precariously placed on satchel belts. It really was too easy. Most wouldn't miss the cards since they had several others along with them. I glanced at the jewels which were shining beneath the glass of a guarded case, locked tightly for security. If I could get my hands on one of those, I could sell it elsewhere and have more than enough to fix my ship and fly away from the planet.

Claire filled my thoughts as I made my way out of Opes and back to the regular part of the great city. The Exchange had a line and I waited patiently. The clerk smiled and nodded when it was my turn.

"Exchange these for a universal card."

She picked up the cards, scanned each one and waited for the amount. My breath held, waiting and hoping that it would be enough to enter the auction house. She slid the card back with the receipt of the amount.

I had to look twice at the amount on the receipt. It was more than enough to purchase a slave as well as to fix the spaceship. My fortunes were already beginning to turn and I hoped that such a thing meant that I would soon find my fated mate.

The city was crammed with more beings waiting on the auction. A low growl came from my throat as I thought about what the aliens would do to Claire if they got her. I was ready to tear out their throats to save her if need be. Dust plumes rose as I approached the road heading toward the auction. Horror filled me when I saw the line of creatures waiting to get inside. It was too long and there were too many of them.

The line moved slowly forward and some were turned around. No doubt, their scanned currency cards didn't hold enough funds to purchase a slave. Finally, my turn came.

"Card," the tall spindly being asked as he bent forward toward me.

I handed the card over and waited while he scanned it. "Proceed."

A weight lifted from me as I entered the private entrance. Still, ahead of me the line continued to move slowly. Lights beamed on the building, which was huge with a giant arena inside. My heart told me that Claire was here, though I had no true evidence of this; other than instinct. This was all new to me, after all. Having a potential mate clouded my mission of simply leaving Reazus. My life and thoughts now centered around the Terran who crashed into my arms.

I stumbled through the crowd, all of them fighting to get inside the great arena. Once I did get in, my ears ached as the crowd shouted wildly for the auction to commence. The auctioneers began the bidding and my heart tumbled within my chest as I hoped to save my mate. I gulped in great bouts of gall as other buyers left with their slaves, the exotics of the Canis Opus System nearby. Glittery females, bedecked in incredible jewels and barely dressed, stepped before their new masters, who literally poked them ahead with sticks or other prods.

My stomach turned at the thought of what they intended with these beautiful beings. Still, I only had one that I hoped to buy. One to rescue from the clutches of a doomed fate.

The crowd continued to push forward through entry gates just before the arena seating. Each guard there held tranquilizer-laced maces in their hands, larger than their heads and sharp enough to pierce through the thickest of skulls. One whack and the opponent went down in a stupor to wait for other guards to drag them off and discard them into the swamps at the side of the building.

The closer I got, the slower the line moved. Within the arena, the auctions continued. Each slave marched out center stage while the crowd shouted their bids. My breath held each time, hoping that it wasn't a Terran named Claire.

The guard stopped me, keeping his giant mace stretched across the doorway. He looked inward, watching the crowd while holding back the ones outside.

"Please, can't I just watch?" I asked.

"No."

It was a short, simple answer that left me ill. The transactions for buying the slaves here happened so quickly. They gathered their purchase and left the auction house with no fuss. No Terrans, however, had left the arena. Convinced that Claire was within, I kept my feet planted firmly at the entrance. The brute alien with the mace wouldn't budge enough to let me slip through, though.

Opportunity presented itself when a scuffle broke out just within the arena and the mace-wielding alien took off to do his duty. I slipped inside, keeping to the shadows and advanced closer to the arena floor. The packed seats clamoured with beings wanting the perfect slave. The announcement came for rare exotics. My breath held as I watched the center of the stage.

CHAPTER 11

CLAIRE

They pushed me toward the edge of the arena. I watched in horror as one after the other of the beautiful females took the stage and were bought by the grubbing lust-filled aliens in the crowd. A cool draft wafted around my barely-covered body. Goosebumps formed across my legs and arms. Oh, to be in Derix's cozy camp, with him nearby. My thoughts went to the moments that he held me on his lap when he saved me from falling. His face remained in my heart, along with his glowing tattoos that revealed his true wishes with me.

"Go!" The guard barked at me, his sharp prod pushing me forward.

I turned with tears in my eyes and realized that it was my turn to take center stage. The guard pushed me hard and I stumbled and fell, landing hard on my knees. The concrete-like floor did little to cushion the fall.

There was no time to cry over it. The guard poked at me again. "Get out there."

The crowd shouted wildly when I stepped into the center of the arena. Bright lights kept me from seeing completely within the crowd. Still, I searched for

Derix, hoping that he'd somehow figured out what had happened to me.

The guard told me to turn, slowly. The crowd yelled when I did, showing off my almost-nude body. Unfortunately, I understood every word uttered thanks to the implant behind my ear. I began to wish that I couldn't understand the aliens. And if ever I had any doubt about being on a planet other than Earth, that was gone now. The alien faces in the crowd gawked at me as if I was a piece of meat and they were starving.

"Healthy, female, Terran, and a genetic match to many in here. Her reproductive organs work, and her body offers the ability to derive pleasure for most."

Horrific words, saying nothing of my intelligence. I bemoaned the microbiology degree I had received. Obviously, my fate centered around keeping some bullish alien male satisfied and bearing his young. Some of the species out there would kill me to carry their babies.

"Oh, Derix," I cried as I peered through the sea of faces to look for the magenta and purple being who looked more human than most of these.

"Turn," the guard growled.

Aliens yelled in their respective languages as the bids came through. Cold air swirled around me, an indication of what lay ahead. It came down to three beings, each one outbidding the other. One of them was a tall, thin-faced creature who looked as if his face was melting. He had large, mis-shapened eyes, a mouth with a permanent frown, and large nostrils that snorted with each bellow of his bid.

Another alien peered at me with beady eyes and a fat face, that billowed with tears. His neck and chin formed the base of his face and the fat rolls continued all the way to his forehead.

A third alien had a breathing device covering his mouth and nose. Puffs of smoke or steam rose with each breath that he took. Judging by the machine strapped to his bicep, he was an ethane breather. Of all, he remained the most calm during the bids.

"Derix, where are you?" I shouted to the crowd. If he were here, he'd surely try to bid for me, even if he didn't have the money to buy me. I'm game for running away. Being claimed by him was far better than what appeared to be my current fate.

Why me? Why was I taken from Earth? My life would never be the same again. I feared that Earth would eventually become a dim memory in the deep recesses of my mind. Even Derix would become my unrequited love if I was sold to one of these beasts.

"Sold to 434," the announcer boomed.

The ethane breather stood to my horror. He grunted as he walked through the crowd to collect his win, me.

"*Derix!*" I screamed as loudly as I could. Please, Derix, save me. With my new fate sealed, the guard pushed me off the center of the arena stage. Large tears blinded my sight as I lost control and stumbled again, down the steps to the back of the arena.

Landing hard on my hands and knees, I desperately looked around while hoping to find a place to hide. Still on my hands and knees, I crawled away through a sea of legs and hoped to slip away. Someone grabbed me, pulling me to my feet roughly. It was a different guard, one that held a giant mace in his hand.

"You go. You're sold." His gruff voice sent shivers through my spine as he shoved me toward a door.

Where was the ethane breather? Where was Derix? Two aliens grabbed my upper arms, moving me through the myriad of halls away from the jeering crowd in the arena. The poor soul standing in the center of the arena as I left undoubtedly felt as scared as I did.

Tears continued to pour from my eyes and seemed unstoppable. I couldn't control the utter bawling as I was being escorted to my new master. How could this have happened to me? I would have given anything to be back with Derix. In fact, my entire being longed for the magenta alien to claim me, to make me his, to protect me.

A hovercraft hummed just outside the door, steam pouring from the stack on top. The ethane breather's driver stepped out and opened the back. His body was every bit as hulking as the one who bought me. What sort of unspeakable things would he want to do to me? I was touted as being a healthy childbearing Terran with a genetic match to most in the arena. Surely, I'm not a complete match to an ethane breather.

I shrugged out of the guards grip, making a run

for the inky night, the darkness showing no indication of what was out there. I didn't care. I'd just as soon a predator eat me than to leave Reazus with the ethane breather. I made it to the edge of the grass and my foot stepped into the swampy water. The sound of a gun going off didn't stop me. I took the chance and ran without looking back. The guard soon caught me and took me by the shoulder to drag me back.

CHAPTER 12

Claire stood in the center of the arena, her body barely covered, her feet bare. I strained to move closer, but the mace-wielding guards stood vigil at every entrance.

My heart pounded when she screamed my name. No one else paid any mind to the exotic's emotions. While the bidding commenced, I looked around for the backstage entrance. The guard stepped to her as she crumbled to the floor, crying. My heart split in two, but I didn't want to draw attention so I merely watched.

She disappeared offstage, and I saw an opening while beings streamed in and out of the hall. I stepped in with the ones heading in, keeping my head down while I moved swiftly toward the back of the auction house.

Up ahead, two guards escorted Claire. She wailed as she stumbled. I thought I heard my name and my heart ached again. If I could call to her, she might not struggle so, but I couldn't risk such a thing.

The back door opened. An aroma of swampy wetness filtered in, the field beyond gleaming in the light of the moon. The occasional cloud blocked the light shrouding the area in thick darkness.

I ran down the hall to another side door that slipped outside, and rushed back around to where they were taking Claire. A hovercraft waited just outside the door. The ethane breather that bought her hadn't shown up yet. His driver, equally a hulking ethane breather, left the vehicle and went inside the building after opening the back door to the craft. It presented the perfect opportunity.

Claire struggled and the guards let go of her long enough for her to run straight for the swamp. On cue, I ran toward them, my dagger out and ready. Before they could grab her, I took hold of one guard and he reeled backward. I overpowered him so quickly that he couldn't struggle as I thrust the dagger deep into his neck. He slumped forward and I dropped him to the ground.

The second guard had no idea what had happened as he lunged for Claire and I pulled my blaster from the harness, pointed it at his back, and fired. The laser cut through his back and his chest, causing him to lose breath immediately. He slumped to the ground, joining his partner just a short distance away. Claire reached the swamp and her foot splashed as I grabbed her. She screamed and I thrust my hand over her mouth and took off to the side where I had parked my own hovercraft.

Claire fought me, and when my hand slipped, she screamed.

"Claire, *shhhh!* It's me, Derix."

Her head cocked around, her eyes wide as she

looked at me.

"*Derix?*" Her voice wavered.

"Be quiet and we'll get out of here before the breather discovers that I killed the guards and grabbed you."

She climbed into my hovercraft and we raced out of the lot near the auction house. There was only one road leading away. Somehow we had to make it out before they stopped us.

"Get down and don't let them see you," I advised as we approached the road leading out.

Guards often stopped traffic as it came through. Earlier, I had to wait in a long line before they would let me through. At this point, there wasn't much traffic left, except for those who bought their slaves. As we approached, the guards received a call on their wrist comms.

The grassy area to the side shone in the partial moonlight. I was certain it wasn't too deep. It was a chance I had to take. Listening intently, I could hear them speaking to the occupants of the vehicle ahead.

"We have an escaped slave. Show your papers," the guard said to them.

"Stay down."

I shoved the vehicle back into hover, the engines humming louder. While the guards were talking with the vehicle in front of me I decided to take the chance. Behind me, the next vehicle slowly came up the road. I didn't wait. Turning sharply, we went into the swampy land, the hover capability keeping the craft just out of the water.

No one came after us, for the guards at the end of the road were on foot. There was no doubt that they'd tell the others which direction we had gone, so I took off in the opposite direction of my camp at first to throw them off.

"You can sit up now," I finally said to the Terran woman.

Claire pulled herself into the seat beside me, her slight body shivering from the cold air swirling around us. We took different roads, turning and leaving no trail for anyone who may have taken off after us.

When we were far enough away, I doubled back, taking a different route around the city back to the camp. We were soon back into the mountains and safe for now. After parking the vehicle within the craggy peaks nearby, we began to walk the rest of the way to the camp.

Claire got out of the hovercraft and flung herself into my arms.

"Oh, Derix, I thought that I'd never see you again," she cried.

I held on as her body shook from the cold and the terrible fear that she had experienced. Her sobs came quickly and I lifted her to me, carrying her the rest of the way through the canyon into my camp.

"I figured you were there. I wasn't going to let any-one take you, Claire. You were dropped into my arms for a reason," I said as I carried her.

Her arms wrapped around my neck tightly.

"Derix, I realized while being held by the pirates that I know where I want to be and that's with you."

We reached the camp and I paused before stepping inside the hideaway. I lifted her chin as I closed the gap between us and we kissed. My heart soared happily as sparks of desire ignited and caused me to want to claim my mate. The only thing I wanted in the galaxy was to make Claire mine.

I set her down as she kept her arms around my neck, tiptoeing backward into the enclosure. Our lips kept moving against each other, our bodies melting together.

CHAPTER 13

Never was I more certain of anything than I was in Derix's arms at that moment. If there was a true reason why I left Earth the way that I did, this must have been it. Every fiber of my being reacted to his touch as he gently laid me onto his pallet. Under the netting and hidden by the overhang of the great boulder, he came down beside me, his body rigid with desire for me.

I turned to him, the smile on my face wouldn't leave. He gazed over me, over the filmy fabric that left nothing to the imagination.

"Are you injured? I saw you fall a couple of times."

"Pain doesn't affect me right now. My heart overpowers it. Skinned knees will heal. My life flashed before me at the arena and that was the worst of it. I saw you in my mind, though at the time I thought of it as a fleeting memory. Now that I'm here in your arms, I don't want to waste another minute. I'm yours, Derix. If you'll have me."

He gingerly lifted the dress over my head, my naked body lying under him. His hands delightfully traced over my curves, gooseflesh chasing along after his touch. I moaned as he leaned forward, his beautiful lips touching mine again. My hands pulled at his clothing.

A low moan rumbled through him as he removed his outfit. Before me under the bits of moonlight flashing above, I explored his muscular body, my fingers tracing over the glowing markings. I gently kissed his chest. Under his colorful warm flesh beat his heart, coming alive with my touch.

Derix groaned as he flipped me around. My arms entwined around neck, his kisses tasting wonderful to me. My body reacted to his gentleness, my legs opening to his rigidity. He moaned as he settled between them both, and I pulled my feet to his lips. Each toe received a kiss, each foot he massaged lovingly with his large hands.

Bending forward, I reached for his bulbous cock, his throbbing member. He lurched forward, groaning with pleasure as my hand rubbed down the girth and over the tip. Small amounts of precum appeared and I gingerly brought my fingers to my lips to taste it.

Derix pulled my pelvis up, his hand on his bulbous cock. He slowly rubbed it through my soft warm folds. I moaned as he slipped inside me, his cock stretching my body around him, and slowly he pressed in all the way. My head rolled back as the sensations both caused pain from the stretching and pleasure from the vibrations.

"Take me," I chanted as he plowed into me harder and faster.

"You're mine, Claire. You're mine." His breaths

came quicker and his moans louder.

I leaned forward, the sensation reaching my clit as he sawed against it. Pleasure flooded my pelvis and exploded. My back arched as I dug my nails into his hips. Derix groaned, moving faster as he breathed harder.

Like fireworks exploding, he burst and emptied into me, the pleasure surging through both of us as the powerful orgasm took hold. I held on for dear life as he pumped into me wildly, his strength overpowering me like nothing else in the world mattered except for what we were doing at that moment.

Completely inebriated by our lovemaking, I fell back onto the pallet, my body pulsating with the remnants of the pleasure that had rocked through me.

Derix soon slowed, his face skewing in utter rapture as he gazed into my face. Very gingerly, he pulled out and laid down to rest beside me, gathering me into his arms.

A hearty sigh escaped his lips, his chest rising contentedly. He wrapped his arms around me as I traced the muscle definition over his well-formed chest.

"My most precious Terran. I will never leave your side now that you are mine. I will fight to the death to keep you safe," he said as he kissed my head.

Contentedness flowed over me like a slow, warm shower. I didn't care that we were at the bottom of a canyon on Reazus. I didn't care what had almost happened to me, though it made me all the more thankful to be in his arms at that moment.

I looked into his eyes, barely seeing the misty white pool surrounding his pupils. "I knew when they captured me what I wanted out of life. There are no regrets from me. With you is where I belong, Derix," I told him as I leaned in and our lips met in a sweet, feathery kiss.

He lifted back, looking into my eyes. "You're happy with me?"

"Of course, I am." I answered.

We slept tangled in each other's arms, our bodies wrapped in the other. When the first sun rose, Derix pulled me to him in a deep kiss. Once again, I gave my body to him, and this time he took me to new heights of pleasure.

"I'm sorry that I lost the shoes." He took a belt and tied it to my feet creating a new pair of shoes for me.

"I'm glad that you're back with me," he replied as he lifted me and we twirled under the heat of the two suns.

"Now, we need to fix your ship so that we can leave this place."

He pulled out a currency card and raised his brow. "This card has enough funds to pay for everything we need for the *Volatus*."

"Seriously? But I'm not about to expose myself to that place again." I shook at the memory that almost became my reality.

"No, there are other places that we can go for the parts we need. We'll head toward the west settlements. It's a longer trip than before, but worth it."

"How long will it take once we have all the parts?"

"About two weeks, maybe three. Then we'll leave Reazus and move on to a safer place."

CHAPTER 14

DERIX

Everything changed after I rescued Claire. Suddenly, my entire world flowed around making her happy and keeping her safe. I no longer cared where we lived, as long as we were together.

"Good news and bad news," I said as I performed the final repair on the *Volatus*.

Claire sighed. "Okay, bad news first." She perched on a rock beside me as I crawled out from the engine bay.

"Bad news, the *Volatus*' hull is so damaged that it needs a new skin and that is something I can't do here."

"Okay, what's the good news, then?" Claire took it better than I had expected.

"It can fly, high in the atmosphere, but not into space."

She grinned. "Then we can fly out of here and to a better place on this planet? A safer place?"

"Yes. I was thinking that we would fill the ship with supplies and find a nice place elsewhere on this planet. It's not all a completely terrible planet."

The excitement of our next adventure energized the air as we loaded the ship with enough supplies to see us through for a month. Where we were going I didn't know.

The *Volatus* lifted from the canyon and straight up into the air. We flew at high speed straight up into the cloud bank, having waited for a cloudy day for better cover.

Claire smiled as she looked through the window. "At least this time, I'm aware of what's going on."

I reached for her and our hands touched, sending warmth up my arm. Every day we would experience it as if it were our first time together. The love between us grew deeper with each passing moment.

The navigation radar showed water below us. I dipped out of the cloud bank, the crystal blue sea below us sparkling from the two suns.

"Is that land?" Claire leaned forward while looking ahead.

We flew to the great rounded treetops on the island. A quick fly around the radius confirmed the place was uninhabited.

"It's perfect, Derix."

Claire bounced on her seat as I landed the ship partially in the water along the shoreline. According to the Reazus map, no one had laid claim on the smaller islands dotted in the sea. It drew excitement from her as we traipsed through the edge of the forest.

"It's like a jungle!" She smiled brighter than the two suns shining overhead.

"We could camp here for a few days and see if we like the area."

CLAIRE

I couldn't believe that it had been four years since we moved to our own little island paradise. Of course, the ship would take us to safer places on the mainland when we needed supplies.

My hand rubbed across my swollen belly. Our first child came a year after we landed on the island, which we named Isle of Amote. Little Iris arrived exactly nine months after we conceived her. She had a beautiful mix of our skin tones as well as my face.

"I want to go back to Earth for a visit once this next baby arrives."

Derix lifted Iris to his lap. "Honestly, Claire, how will they react to us?"

My eyes swung down. "I don't know. Earth might not be ready for this. I just feel terrible that my family thinks I'm in a jungle on Earth and they're awaiting my arrival back home."

"We can relay a message."

Derix had told me before that we could do such a thing if we flew to the nearest relay station. Earth wasn't likely ready for aliens.

After our son, Aetox, arrived, we sent word through some mutual friends who were flying out. We had met another Terran during our excursions to the mainland who had hooked up with her rescuer alien. Both of us had a lot in common.

We returned with our daughter and son, and Derix pulled me onto his lap once the kids were sound asleep.

"Are you happy here with me?"

I turned to him, my arms wrapping around his neck. "I'm the happiest woman in the Milky Way Galaxy. Why would you ask such a thing?"

"I know you wanted to go back to Earth." We locked eyes.

"Derix, I would love to introduce you and the children to my family, but I know that's not possible. Regardless, I choose life with you and with our children. I give myself to you wholeheartedly. I have no regrets."

The tears in his eyes touched me in a way that I knew no human man could have touched me. I meant it when I said I had no regrets. This was home. Forever.

EDEN EMBER

Eden Ember found her passion in writing sci-fi romance. She spends her days either pounding on the keyboard or dreaming up the next stories. Her active imagination never lets up and the perfect outlet comes through in her books.

Join Eden Ember's exclusive reader's list
at EdenEmber.com

OUTLAW PLANET MATES

Don't miss out on the rest of the series! They are standalone books and can be read in any order.

Alien's Mercy - Leslie Chase
Alien's Treasure - Elin Wyn
Alien's Jewel - Ava York
Alien's Challenge - Nancey Cummings
Alien's Stone Heart - Lynnea Lee
Alien's Fate - Eden Ember
Alien's Sacrifice - Cady Austin
Alien's Bounty - Lena Grey
Alien's Surrender - Harper Rosling

And check out The Hub reader's group on Facebook for news about the rest of the series: https://www.facebook.com/groups/854826322125572